Dear Kathy,
this is just a little
something to say "the ["
for taking time to
Grandma. I know she
forward to your
It's comforting to
that she has such
neighbor and friend.
In Christ's love,
Sandi Robert

"Elm Street. The sign silently mocked Peter as it urged him to ride down her street and visit the parsonage and its inhabitants: his mother—held like a prisoner in her own home; Kathryn—torn between her devotion to her nephew's step-son and her loyalty to the master of the house, Rev. Mooring; James—the quiet butler who had always managed to stay out of the family quarrels; and Rev. Mooring—the man who hated him."

Seventy Times Seven

by Sandi Zimmerman Rebert

BOB JONES UNIVERSITY PRESS
Greenville, South Carolina 29614

Seventy Times Seven
by Sandi Zimmerman Rebert

©1982 Bob Jones University Press
Greenville, South Carolina 29614

Printed in the United States of America.
ISBN 0-89084-156-X

To my pastor-husband,
Brian,
for his love,
dedication to God's work,
and encouragement in writing this book.

Chapter 1

Drip, drip, drip. It was a slow, lazy-day rain falling from an overcast sky. Peter parted the lush velvet curtains of the huge library window and glanced out. The gray, cloud-scattered atmosphere was thick and murky. A chill swept over him, causing him to shudder, although he wasn't certain if it were really caused by the weather or the dreaded task that lay ahead of him.

Wearily, he left his post at the window, walked over to the fireplace and threw a log onto the burning embers. Then he sank down into the big, over-stuffed armchair, his stepfather's favorite.

His stepfather—if he could only share with him what was on his heart. Over and over again Peter had rehearsed what he would say; exactly what phrases he would use, the perfect line of reasoning, facial expressions, gestures. Yet, he knew it would

1

be to no avail. He had been waiting, too, ever since last Friday when his soul had nearly been set on fire, for the perfect time to talk to that austere gentleman. Now was as good a time as any. The fire was already beginning to die within him.

He glanced at the log he had cast on the fire. It had begun to turn into glowing ashes. "That's what will become of my dream," he thought, "if I wait any longer, and yet . . ."

A deep sigh escaped his lips. Tossing his head back on the high, comfortable chair and poising his hands thoughtfully under his chin, he stared at the intricate designs on the white, metal ceiling. If only his own father were still alive. He would understand. He would want this for his son.

"I must do it now!" Peter exclaimed, pounding his fist on the arm of the chair. A spirit and energy he had not experienced since Friday surged through his mind and body. Jumping up from his chair, he grabbed a log from the woodpile and boldly tossed it into the fire, along with a second, and a third; then he stepped back as the flames leaped into the air.

"There!" he cried victoriously. "I'll not let it die! 'If God be for me, who can be against me?'" He bowed his head, and clenching his fists tightly, prayed with a fervency beyond his young years. "Oh, Heavenly Father, help me just now. Give me grace, dear Lord, give me grace." Unclenching his fists and giving an imploring look heavenward, he walked over to the massive library table and picked up his well-worn Bible.

"Courage, Peter," he muttered to himself as he clutched the Book close to his heart, "courage."

◆   ◆   ◆

"Who is it?" the gruff, powerful voice boomed from behind the study doors answering Peter's tremulous knock. He was right; it was the wrong time. "I said, who is it?"

"It's me, sir, Peter," he replied, trying to sound as bold as he dared.

A thumping of feet, a steady twist of the knob, and the door opened, revealing a tall, distinguished-looking gentleman who seemed to take in all of Peter's being with one, haughty, distasteful sneer.

Peter winced under his gaze. If only he did not have to face him. Perhaps he should have run away. But he had felt that this was what the Lord would have him do—at least at first.

"Well?" one large, graying eyebrow arched above the other. "If you have something to say, boy, say it! If not, then begone with you! I have work to do!"

"I—I want to talk with you, sir."

There was a long, sickening silence.

Perhaps he should have gone to his mother, but he knew she would have only sent him to see his stepfather. Everything must be cleared through him. He demanded it.

"So, talk, boy!"

Never in the ten years that Peter's mother had been married to this man had he ever referred to Peter by his rightful name or even called him son.

"I wanted to sit down and talk, sir. It might take awhile. It's very important."

"Oh, I see. And you think you can just come to my study any time of the day and make yourself right at home, do you?"

"Well, I—"

"I'm a very busy man, boy. You know that no one, not even your mother, is to bother me when I am studying. You are aware that I spend the entire day on Saturday preparing my sermons. You had no business even disturbing me! I don't care how important you think it is. I haven't time to listen to teenage jabberings!"

Rev. Mooring started to close the door, then, as if reading Peter's mind, added, "And if you wish to speak to me of your future plans, you needn't bother. I have already decided what they shall be, and I will discuss it with you at my convenience. But as for now, I must continue working on my sermon. I don't expect to have such interruptions again! Do you understand?"

Peter knew that whenever his stepfather asked, "Do you understand?" that it was more of a threat than a question. Yet, he also knew that his stepfather expected an answer; a polite, respectful, "Yes, sir."

Gritting his teeth together, Peter managed to emit the proper response. The door closed with a bang.

"I suppose you're going to preach on brotherly love!" Oh, how he wanted to shout it at him! "What a hypocrite!" Peter glared at the door, daring himself to speak the words that were uppermost in his mind. "What do you know of the Bible?" his heart cried out. His eyes were moist with the tears he fought to keep back, his mouth dry, his legs limp.

Staggering to his room, he threw himself across the huge oak bed. If only he'd said it; if only he had walked right in, stated his purpose, and left. Why did he need to ask "him" anyway? The Rev. Thomas Mooring was not his father. What right did he have to order his life? He had not even wanted to give Peter his last name after he and Peter's mother had married.

"I wish I'd called him a hypocrite right to his face," Peter thought ruefully, although deep down he was rather relieved that he hadn't. He had experienced the sting of his stepfather's strong hand across his face before. He had no desire to add that injury to the insults he had already endured.

Emotionally exhausted and soul-sick, Peter fell asleep.

Chapter 2

The flickering candlelight sent dancing shadows across the long mahogany table. The silverware sparkled, the china shone brightly, and the delicious aroma of food permeated the room.

Rev. Mooring tapped his fingers nervously on the table. "Where is that boy of yours, Nancy?"

"You mean, Peter, dear?" she answered softly from the other end of the long table, subtly emphasizing the "Peter." How deeply it hurt her to hear him call her only child—her son—"boy," as if he were a servant. Yet, she dare not make her feelings known. She, too, had sustained the temper of the Rev. Thomas Mooring.

"You know who I mean! Why isn't he at dinner?"

"I don't know, dear."

"Well, I do," piped in Kathryn, Rev. Mooring's petite spinster aunt, as she entered the room with the tea service filled with the special herb tea the Reverend always drank with his dinner.

"No one asked you, Aunt Kathryn, and you were eavesdropping, weren't you?" Rev. Mooring stated in a severe voice, squinting his already narrow eyes at her.

"No, Thomas, no one did ask me, and yes, I was eavesdropping," she replied just as emphatically. If there was anyone who was not afraid to speak her mind, even to the Rev. Mooring, it was Kathryn. Perhaps it was because she was his late father's sister, or the fact that she was the Reverend's only living relative that permitted her to say things to his face that others dared not think in his presence.

"Well," he huffed, "since you know so much, then, where is he? Why haven't you called him?"

Unaffected by the blame suddenly being cast upon her, Kathryn carefully poured the tea in his cup and handed it to him.

"Well, when I realized that Peter wasn't coming down for dinner, I not only called him, I went myself to see where he was and what could be wrong with him. I knew something must be amiss, because I know how dearly that boy loves to eat!" Kathryn also had a knack for making a short story long and a long story even longer.

"Please get to the point!"

"Very well, Thomas. He is in his room fast asleep, and I didn't have the heart to awaken him."

"He's not sick, is he, Kathryn?" Nancy Mooring inquired anxiously.

"Oh, no, dear. He's not sick." She cast a knowing look at the Reverend.

"What does she mean, Thomas? Do you know?"

"It's nothing, Nancy."

"Oh, I don't know that I would say that."

"Aunt Kathryn!" Mr. Mooring rose from his place, his face crimson with anger. "You have said more than enough! This matter is between Peter and myself and does not concern you in the least! I'll thank you to keep out of my business!"

"All right, all right, Thomas. No need to shout. I'm leaving." The older lady puttered off to the kitchen shaking her head sadly and muttering under her breath. "I never in my life saw such a temper. That man's going to give himself a heart attack one of these days."

Except for the constant patter of rain on the windows, the room was quiet after Kathryn had disappeared into the friendly recluse of the kitchen.

Nancy Mooring stared at her plate, inwardly yearning to go upstairs and draw her son to herself as she had when he was young, rocking him in her arms as he poured out his childish burdens to her, and then magically melting them all away with a mother's kiss. She sighed, not realizing that it was audible, and thought of happier times when her Jonathan was still alive. A simple, God-fearing preacher of a little loving congregation; she the patient, good-hearted wife and mother; and little Peter, their little Peter, the exact image of his father.

She fingered the delicate water goblet in front of her. Ah, how things had changed! Jonathan dead—brutally murdered by a drunk he was trying to bring to the Savior, the loneliness and hatred she had felt, the resentment towards God, the whirlwind courtship with Rev. Mooring—one of the richest and most highly esteemed men in all of Philadelphia, the big wedding in his impressive church, the beautiful parsonage, the silk and velvet dresses, rich furniture, servants—everything she had ever dreamed about as a girl.

Now the dream had dulled. Thomas Mooring was not the man she had thought him to be. Now, it was too late. Peter was eighteen, almost a man. Where had the years gone? What had she done to her beloved son?

Her thoughts were interrupted by a clatter of silverware on the china.

"I know what you're thinking, Nancy!" the Reverend said fiercely. "You think I've done something to hurt *your* boy. Well, I haven't! He's acting like a child! First, he interrupted me at my studies, and now he's interrupting our dinner! I'm going upstairs and have a talk with him!"

"Please, Thomas," she started to rise from her seat, "maybe I'd better talk to him."

"I'm the man of this house; I'll talk to him!"

How that look in his eyes frightened her; yet, she knew his words were final. She sank back into her chair. As soon as she could hear the sound of his shoes on the stairs, she pushed her plate away and, folding her arms on the table, laid her head down and sobbed.

Out of nowhere, frail, sympathetic arms gently enfolded her shaking shoulders, and loving hands stroked her long golden hair.

"It is all right, dear. You just cry," Kathryn said softly.

◆　◆　◆

The violent pounding awakened Peter with a start.

"Who is it?" he whispered hoarsely.

The door flung open and banged against the wall.

"Get up!"

Peter cringed at the sight of him. The Reverend's eyes were blazing with fury. Peter knew he must obey or suffer the consequences of one of his stepfather's fits of rage. Wondering what he had done now, he quickly rose to his feet.

"Why weren't you at dinner?"

"I—I guess I must have fallen asleep, sir. I didn't know it was time for dinner."

"You have ruined my appetite and your mother's, and caused her to question my authority and handling of your matters, as well as put the entire household in an uproar!"

Peter blinked in astonishment at all the trouble he had managed to cause while sleeping. It almost made him feel like laughing—but his stepfather didn't seem to find it humorous. The big man took several strides toward Peter. Instinctively, Peter stepped backward. He felt the edge of the bed against his leg.

"Please, sir, I—I didn't mean to cause any trouble. Honest, sir."

"Well, see that you don't cause any more. Do you understand?" He grabbed Peter's collar. Peter swallowed hard. "And I don't want one word mentioned to your mother about this afternoon, not one word, boy, or you'll deal with this!" He raised back his hand as if to strike Peter. Peter drew his head back, bracing himself for the blow—but it never came.

Rev. Mooring released Peter from his grip and moved towards the door. "You'll be seated at the table in two minutes!"

"Yes, sir," came the meek reply.

Chapter 3

It was Sunday. During the early morning, the sun had peeped through the clouds, chasing away the gray fog, until the day had blossomed into a beautiful, tranquil picture.

Peter squirmed in his seat. He hadn't planned to be at church this morning—at least not this one. Several times during the night he had gathered a few belongings together and wrapped them in a blanket, planning to silently escape down the back stairs and out into the night: away from his stepfather, away from the rich surroundings he had grown to hate, away from the hypocrisy of high society. But thoughts of his dear mother had caused him to remain, and now he knew he must somehow force himself to sit through another one of his stepfather's orations.

That was all it amounted to, Peter told himself. This man behind the pulpit knew nothing of the Savior. Oh, his sermons were full of flowery words and picturesque phrases that made his prestigious audience feel quite pleased with themselves and extremely self-righteous. But they contained nothing of the fiery fervency of a heart yielded to God, a heart burning with a steadfast desire to glorify the Lord and win lost souls to Calvary.

The choir was beginning their last song before the message, something by Bach, he vaguely heard. But Peter wasn't listening to the choir, or the beautiful sonorous notes from the pipe organ. His mind was painting a scene of bygone years: of a little chapel out in the country, a few bedraggled farmers and housewives, a drunk, and a couple of society's misfits.

At an old, worn-out piano sat a lovely lady with long, golden curls. She smiled sweetly back at him in the front row. His heart throbbed. He wanted to throw her a kiss, but he would have been embarrassed in front of all those people. Besides, he was seven now, and getting to be too old for such things.

The congregation had just finished singing a simple chorus full of meaning—"Amazing grace, how sweet the sound, that saved a wretch like me."

The preacher got up behind the rickety pulpit and opened his tattered little Bible, dog-eared and marred from years of fond use. It was hard for Peter to see his face. He squinted to see better, but it was only a blurred memory. He could hear the preacher's voice, though, loud and clear, full of divine urgency and love.

"The topic I have chosen for today is well-fitting to be given in this centennial year in our fair city of Philadelphia, for it is the subject of—brotherly love."

The dream shattered. Instead of the little chapel, Peter found himself seated inside the ornate First Church of Philadelphia. The congregation had turned into professors, doctors, bankers, lawyers, and other well-known professionals and socialites of the day. The old piano had been replaced with a magnificent organ. The lovely lady was still there, but she was seated beside him on the blue velvet covered pew. He glanced sideways at her. She seemed so much older than he had remembered.

Finally, he shifted his eyes to the preacher, a distinguished, well-poised gentleman in his prime, the premature gray at his temples only adding to the appearance of refinement. His clothes bore not a wrinkle. He smiled cordially at his audience. His gestures were practiced and precise. His words were dripping with honey and—

"Hypocrisy!" Before Peter realized it, the word had escaped his lips. He'd shouted it—he'd stood up and shouted it right in the middle of his stepfather's sermon!

A hush fell over the congregation as all eyes riveted their attention upon him. Peter dared not look at anyone, especially his stepfather, though he could feel those narrow eyes piercing right through him with their fiery darts.

He hadn't meant to say it—only think it! Not even daring to look at his mother, Peter stumbled over the obese man at the end of the aisle and dashed out the closest door.

His heart throbbed. Afraid that his stepfather might send one of the ushers after him, he continued running until he had reached the kitchen door of the parsonage a block and a half away. Dazed and breathless, he threw the door open and plunged onto one of the plank bottom chairs.

"Why, Peter, whatever is wrong with you?" exclaimed Kathryn, almost dropping the pan of bread she had just removed from the brick oven. "You're as white as a ghost!"

Peter stared straight ahead. He was panting. His legs throbbed and his heart ached.

"I did it, Nanna! I did it!" From the moment Peter had first laid eyes on Kathryn as a lonely, fatherless boy of ten, he had called her Nanna, and the special position the thin, white-haired lady had captured in his heart then had never diminished.

"Did what, Peter? What is wrong?" She felt his forehead with the back of her hand.

Peter pushed her hand away violently and got up. He began pacing back and forth across the kitchen. "I didn't mean to do it, Nanna!" He gestured wildly with his hands.

"That's all right, Peter. I forgive you."

"No, no, you don't understand!" He stood directly in front of her, a frightened look in his eyes.

"Peter, have you gone crazy?"

"No! Yes! No! Maybe I have!"

"Here," she gently took him by the shoulders and pushed him towards the chair. "You just sit down on this chair and calm yourself. Then you tell your old Nanna all about it."

"No!" He wheeled around at her with a force that half startled, half frightened her. "I can't! I have to go!"

"Go? Go where?"

"I don't know. Anywhere but here! I have to go before he gets here!"

"He? Who's he? Peter, you're not making any sense." But Peter didn't answer her. He was already past her and half way up the stairs. "What is the matter with that boy? You'd think he'd seen the devil himself!" she muttered to herself as she hobbled as fast as she could up the rickety back staircase.

When she finally reached Peter's room at the end of the hall, she was gasping for breath. "I'm getting too old for such games, Peter."

Peter was frantically getting clothes out of the highboy and throwing them on the bed.

"What are you doing, child?"

"I'm leaving." He grabbed the top blanket out of the blanket-chest and spread it on the floor, then started dumping the clothes from the bed onto it.

"Now you look here, young man—" It had been a long time since Kathryn had called him "young man" in that stern kind of voice she had used when he was a little boy about to stick his finger in the chocolate frosting of the cake she had just baked. "You're not going anywhere until you tell Nanna what's wrong with you."

"I don't have time, Nanna! You'll find out soon enough—after I'm gone." As he tied up the corners of the blanket together, he looked up at the beloved woman. With a trembling hand she wiped away the tear that had escaped and trickled down her wrinkled cheek. He had an impulse to hug her, but then he would break down and tell her the whole story, and he knew there wasn't time. Every second counted.

"Tell—tell mother I love her," he choked back the tears, "and I'll let her know where I am."

As he reached down to pick up his bundle, Peter heard a loud thumping noise on the stairs. A sharp, stabbing pain shot through him. It was too late!

Chapter 4

"Just where do you think you're going?" The voice boomed like thunder. Peter felt his knees grow weak.

"Please, Thomas," came a broken, pleading voice from the bottom of the staircase. "Please don't hurt him! He didn't mean to do it. Please!" His mother's voice broke into half-stifled sobs.

Unmoved by his wife's entreaties, Rev. Mooring thundered into the room.

"What's going on here? What are you going to do?" Kathryn questioned helplessly.

"Out, Kathryn!"

"Thomas, you're not going to hurt him."

"Out!"

"Thomas, please, listen to me. You're beside yourself."

"Get out!" he shouted, pointing a long finger towards the door. "I'll not tell you again!" He swore at her.

Without another word, Kathryn was gone, and the door slammed behind her.

"Look at me, boy!"

Slowly, Peter lifted his eyes from his

bundle, which, up until this point, he had not dared to look away from, and met his stepfather's icy glare.

Rev. Mooring stood stiff and erect, towering even above Peter's five feet, ten inches. His face was burning with rage. He was breathing heavily.

Peter tried to speak, but the words caught in his throat. He wanted to run, but there was nowhere to go. All he could do was stand there, trembling, gazing into those sharp daggers that pierced his soul. He felt sick. If only he could faint.

"Thought you'd get away before I came home, did you?" Rev. Mooring half thundered, half snickered.

Peter said nothing.

"Well, you're not going to get off that easy, boy." He smirked sadistically, as if he were thoroughly going to enjoy the punishment he was about to bestow. "Do you hear? You're going to pay for what you've done to me!"

The back of his hand caught Peter across the face. Stunned, Peter staggered backwards, placing his hand in front of his face to ward off another blow. He could hear his mother and Kathryn crying outside the door.

"Please—please, sir, let me explain," he gulped.

"Let you explain," the Reverend repeated sarcastically. "Let me explain, boy!

You've ruined me! Ruined me, do you understand!" Another slap and Peter stumbled over the leg of the bed.

"Do you know who was in that service, boy? Do you?" His screaming made Peter's ears ring.

"No—no, sir."

"Well, I'll tell you, boy!" He grabbed Peter by the collar. This time Peter knew he would not be loosed. "There were administrators there, boy! Administrators from Harvard! Harvard University, boy!"

He was leaning over Peter, breathing out every word like fire.

"And do you know *why* they were there, boy?" Peter's collar tightened around his throat.

"N—no, sir," he gasped.

"They were here to listen to my preaching, to consider me for a teaching position at Harvard, boy! Harvard!" His grip on Peter's collar grew even tighter.

"P—please, sir, you're choking me." Peter grabbed his stepfather's hands and tried to pry them away from his throat, but the big man was stronger than he.

"They'll be here any minute to interview me, boy! What are they going to say? 'Was that your boy who stood up and called you a hypocrite?' Hypocrite! That's what you called me! Hypocrite! Right in front of the whole church!"

Rev. Mooring's free hand came crashing down so hard this time that it sent Peter sprawling to the floor. Peter's head swam. His throat felt raw. His face stung sharply. He felt something coming from his mouth and wiped it away with his hand—blood. If only the floor would swallow him up.

"Dear, Lord," he prayed silently, "help me!" Supporting himself on one hand, he tried to get up, but was too weak.

"You've ruined me!" His stepfather's eyes were flashing wildly with hatred. Peter could see he wasn't through with him yet.

Rev. Mooring grabbed Peter's collar again. "Get up, boy!" He jerked Peter to his knees.

"Reverend Mooring, sir!" There was a fierce pounding on the bedroom door. It flew open to reveal James, the butler. James stared down at Peter, then at Reverend Mooring. His eyes were wide with excitement, though he managed to retain the proper dignity for his position.

"What do you want?!"

"They're here, sir. The men from Harvard."

Momentarily stunned, Rev. Mooring breathed deeply several times to regain his composure. It wouldn't do for them to see him like this. He must be at his best when they interviewed him.

"Tell them—tell them I'll be there in a

few minutes."

"Yes, sir." James gave Peter a sympathetic look, then left the room, closing the door behind him.

Rev. Mooring turned back towards Peter and glared at him. "You'd better pray I get that job, boy!"

He released Peter with a quick jerk and moved towards the door. "And don't think you can run away, either," he added, as he put his hand on the knob and gave it a quick twist.

The door closed once again, but this time Peter heard the click of the key in the lock.

Chapter 5

Dizzy and weak, Peter remained on his knees for a few seconds in stunned silence, then, reaching for the bed post, hoisted himself up and fell exhausted onto the feather-stuffed mattress. It seemed like hours that he stayed in that semi-conscious position, when he heard the key click in the lock again.

A low moan escaped his lips. He wasn't

ready for more. He couldn't endure another beating—not now. He wished he were dead.

The door creaked open. Peter strained to open his eyes, but the right one was almost swollen shut.

"Peter!"

"Oh, my dear!"

The two women spoke in excited whispers.

"Aunt Kathryn, will you chip off some ice from the block in the icebox and put it in a washcloth for me please?"

"Of course, dear. I'll be right back."

"Oh, Peter," his mother was beside him now, stroking his thick blond hair. "Oh, my darling, I'm so sorry!"

"I—I didn't mean to do it, Mother. I was daydreaming."

"I know, dear. Please don't think about it. Besides, what you said was the truth. Perhaps it should have been said long ago." Her voice trailed off wistfully.

Peter started to get up. His mother helped him to the edge of the bed.

"Here's the ice. Thomas is still talking with those gentlemen."

"Good," replied Nancy, applying the cold compress to Peter's swollen face. "We don't have much time. Peter," she turned his face toward her, "this teaching position is very important to your stepfather. If he doesn't get it, there's no telling what he'll do."

23

"I know."

"You've got to get away, at least for a few days, until his anger has subsided."

Peter nodded silently. He looked at her through his one good eye. How beautiful she was, how good—his own dear mother. Somehow, he knew it would be more than a few days until he saw her face again.

Nancy Mooring was thinking the same thing, for she hastily brushed away a tear that had fallen down her smooth cheek, forced a smile, and said brightly, "Perhaps —perhaps he'll get the job after all, and then everything will be all right."

Peter forced a weak smile, then threw his arms around her neck and hugged her passionately. Both mother and son longed to release the tears they fought so hard to hold back, but there would be plenty of time for tears later.

"Nancy! Nancy!" Kathryn dashed into the room from her post at the hallway banister. "They're getting ready to leave!"

Now that Peter knew he had just a few minutes to escape, the adrenalin shot through his body, giving him renewed strength. Quickly, he picked up his bundle.

"We'll go down the back stairs and out the kitchen door," Nancy whispered as they tip-toed down the hall. "There's a horse tethered for you outside. You'll have to go down the back alley."

When they reached the kitchen, Kathryn grabbed another bundle. "Food," she said simply.

The two women followed Peter outside and strapped the bundles to the horse's back as Peter mounted.

"Where will you go, son?"

"To the mission on the south side of town." He had already planned that the night before.

"I'll send messages to you through Kathryn. No doubt your stepfather will be watching me closely so I dare not leave for a while."

Just then they heard the crack of a whip and the sound of carriage wheels on the cobblestone.

"Oh, hurry, Peter!" Aunt Kathryn was beside herself with excitement.

"God go with you, my son!" Peter felt some bills being pressed into his hand. He leaned over and kissed his mother goodbye. Then, spurring the horse as hard as he could, he galloped down the alley.

Chapter 6

Peter sat on the hard wooden bench with his head between his hands.

"Still no word from your mother?"

He looked up into the sympathetic eyes of Rev. Carlson, the pastor of the little rescue mission which had been Peter's home for almost a week.

"No, sir, nothing."

"Don't despair, son." Oh, how good that simple word sounded to his ears—son. "Do you still believe in Romans 8:28?" Rev. Carlson added, smiling.

"I guess so," Peter replied dejectedly.

Rev. Carlson shook his head. "No, you don't, or you wouldn't be moping around yet after a whole week has gone by," he added kindly but firmly.

Peter lurched out of his seat. "What do you know about it?" he cried, his eyes flashing. "What do you know about having a stepfather who hates you? What do you know about maybe never seeing your mother again?" He leaned against the window pane and looked out, biting his lips to keep from screaming, or crying, or both.

"I know something about it, Peter," came the soft reply. "You see, I was brought up in an orphanage."

"I—I'm sorry, sir." Peter pressed his head against the side of the window and sobbed.

"That's it, son, let it out." Rev. Carlson gently patted him on the back. "It's good for a body to release all that tension sometimes. The good Lord gave us tears for a reason. I'll leave you for awhile. You and I can have a good talk tonight after supper. All right?"

Peter nodded. Rev. Carlson patted him on the back again, then disappeared behind the curtain and up the stairs that led to his and Mrs. Carlson's little apartment.

As soon as he heard the upstairs door click shut, Peter pounded his fist into the wall. "Why?" his heart cried out. "Why must it be like this? Why haven't I heard from her?" Angrily, he looked at the ceiling, tears streaming down his face. "Sure, I believe everything works together for good," he wanted to shout, "for everyone but me!" He leaned against the pane once more, this time sobbing uncontrollably until his shoulders shook and his head ached.

"Peter?"

Peter sniffed back the tears. Had he heard right? Was it really—

"Peter? Are you all right?"

"Nanna?" He wheeled around. "Nanna! Oh, Nanna!" He caught her hands in his and pressed them tightly. "Is it really you?"

"Well, I don't know who else I'd be."

"Oh, Nanna, you don't know how glad I am to see you!" He pulled her over to a bench and they sat down. "Tell me everything that's happened."

Kathryn cocked her head and looked at him askance. "You were crying, weren't you, Peter?"

Realizing what a sight he must be, Peter quickly rubbed his shirt sleeve across his eyes. "Course not!" he answered, a sly grin on his face. "Oh, tell me, how is mother?"

"Your mother is fine. Why were you crying, Peter? They aren't treating you poorly, are they?" She nodded towards the upstairs.

"No, of course not. Please—tell me—"

"Then why is my boy crying?"

"Nanna—oh," he cried exasperatedly. He knew she would never be satisfied until she had all the particulars. "If you really must know, it was because of you."

"Me?"

"Yes."

"What did I do to hurt you?" she asked sincerely.

"Nothing. It's just that—oh, Nanna, where have you been? Every day I've watched for you. I nearly went crazy wondering what had happened to you and mother. I thought you might never come!"

"Well, I'll be! Is that all?" As if his days of anxiety had been nothing. She was the same old Kathryn.

"Yes," he laughed, "that's all." Oh, how good it felt to laugh. "Now, please," his deep blue eyes pleaded with her, "tell me what's happened."

"Well, I hardly know where to begin."

"Just start at the beginning. Did he get the job?"

"Your stepfather?" she snorted. "No, he didn't get the job."

Peter's eyes fell. "Was it because of me?"

"They didn't say why, just that they didn't feel he was the right one for the position."

"Is that what he told you?"

"No. He says it's because of you. But I know better. I saw the letter they sent him." She grinned sheepishly.

He smiled back. Leave it to Kathryn.

"Then he didn't find out on Sunday?"

"No, dear, he didn't find out until yesterday. That's why I waited until today to come." She patted his hand good-naturedly. "You see, Peter, we didn't forget you."

Peter glanced away from her. "Was he —was he awfully mad when he found out I was gone?"

"Was he ever! I never saw him so mad as

29

he was that day! And believe me, I've seen him pretty mad!"

"Was he angry at me, or you and mother?"

"He was mad at everybody! He swore like a sailor and stomped around like a little child having a temper tantrum. My dear brother would have been ashamed of him."

"He didn't—" Peter bit his lip. "He didn't hit her, did he?"

"No, child, he didn't hit her." She glanced away from him as if there were more to tell that she would rather not say. Peter guessed at her silence.

"And you?"

Her eyes met his and held his gaze for a minute, then dropped as she quickly brushed away a tear.

"He didn't! How could he?" Peter rose from his seat.

"I wasn't going to tell you, unless you asked. But it's all right, dear."

"It's not all right!" Peter crossed the room to the podium that Rev. Carlson used for a pulpit. "It's all my fault!" He pounded it with his fist. "I never should have left. I should have taken what was coming to me!"

"No, Peter, don't ever say that!" Kathryn was standing behind him now. "He probably would have killed you, or come close to it. I never would have thought I'd see the day that he would strike me. I fear for him, Peter.

His temper will be his downfall, just you wait and see. But please, dear, don't worry about it. Everything will work out for the best, you'll see."

"So I've been told," he muttered.

Slowly, he turned around and faced her. "I — I guess that means I won't be coming home, doesn't it."

"Yes, dear," her voice was full of emotion. "I guess it does."

A long silence passed between them.

"Your mother—she worries about you. She's not sure you're getting enough to eat, or have a nice comfortable bed." Kathryn gazed around at the plain, dismal surroundings.

"She doesn't have to worry about that, Nanna. Rev. Carlson and his wife have been very good to me. I couldn't want for anything more except ..." He swallowed hard.

"That's all right, dear. I understand."

Kathryn put the hood of her cape over her head and started to leave.

"Nanna," he said, stopping her.

"Yes, Peter?"

"Tell," he took a deep breath, "when will I see you again?"

"Probably next Friday, dear. It wouldn't be good for me to be gone too many times. He might start asking questions."

Peter nodded.

Watching her out the window until the hooded figure disappeared behind an old

31

brick building, he whispered hoarsely, "Tell mother—I love her."

Chapter 7

It was an undeniable fact that Martha Carlson was a good cook, concocting sumptuous meals out of the most meager fare. And this evening was no exception.

"Well, Peter," John Carlson remarked, wiping his mouth with the corner of his napkin, "the Lord didn't forget you after all, did He?" There was a merry twinkle in his eyes.

"No, sir," Peter blushed, "I guess He didn't. About this afternoon, sir—"

"No apology necessary, son. I know exactly how you felt. I've been there many times myself. Self-pity—it's a tool of the devil, and he knows how to use it well."

"How is your mother, Peter?" Mrs. Carlson ventured.

"Fine, ma'am. I wish you could meet her." His voice trailed off wistfully.

"I'm sure she's a fine lady." Mrs. Carlson smiled at him sweetly.

Seeing that it was time to change the subject, Rev. Carlson loudly cleared his throat. "Here, Peter, have some more corn."

◆ ◆ ◆

As soon as supper was finished, Martha Carlson began clearing the table. Peter watched her admiringly. She was a pleasant woman, a little too round for her height, but not exactly what he would call fat—more like pleasingly plump. Her long gray-black hair was tied back in a bun, a few thin wisps falling delicately around her face. She was the perfect complement to John Carlson, as soft-spoken and sweet as he was outspoken and frank. His mother would look a little like her someday.

"Well, Peter," Mr. Carlson's loud voice broke in on his thoughts. "While the Missus is doing the dishes, why don't you and I have our little talk I promised this afternoon?" He pointed to the davenport. "Shall we?"

Peter rose from his chair. "Yes, sir. That was a very delicious meal, Mrs. Carlson. Thank you."

"Oh, Peter," she chuckled, "You needn't thank me every night. I might get spoiled!"

"I don't think anything could ever spoil you, ma'am. Besides," he looked from one to the other, "you don't know what it means to me—the two of you taking me in like this—treating me as if I were your own—son."

Martha Carlson looked lovingly at her husband, then at Peter. Mr. Carlson cleared his throat. "Well, Peter, Mrs. Carlson and I almost feel as if you were our son."

"You see, Peter," Mrs. Carlson added softly, "we never had any children of our own," her voice broke with emotion, "so you're really an answer to prayer." She brushed away a tear and smiled, then turned back to her dishes.

"Humph." Rev. Carlson cleared his throat again. It seemed that it was the only bridge he knew to escape from an over-emotional situation back to the business at hand.

Motioning for Peter to have a seat, he disappeared into the little bedroom and returned with his Bible.

"Why don't we have a word of prayer to begin with?" he said as he sat down on the worn-out couch. "Dear Lord, we know that our times are in Your hands, and that the steps of a good man are ordered by the Lord. We pray just now that you would give special wisdom and grace to young Peter here, and that You would use him mightily for Your honor and glory. Be with his dear mother, Lord, and comfort her heart, and may they be reunited soon, if it be Thy will. In Jesus' name, Amen."

"Thank you, sir," Peter whispered, running his finger absent-mindedly over the flowered pattern of the sofa cushion.

"Humph. Now then, Peter, how would you like to preach for me next Sunday?"

"Preach, sir?" Peter gulped.

"Yes. You feel the Lord is calling you to preach, don't you?"

"Well, yes, sir, that is, I—"

"As I recall, you dedicated your life to Him for just that purpose only—let's see—why, two weeks ago, right here in our little mission."

"Well, yes, sir—but—"

"So I see no reason why you shouldn't begin at once."

Peter glanced helplessly at Mrs. Carlson. She was still busy with the dishes, but he thought he detected a slight smile playing at the corner of her lips.

"But sir, I never preached before!"

"Of course, you haven't. But there's always a first time for everything."

"Will you help me?"

"Help you! My dear boy, you had best start right from the beginning to get your sermons from the Lord, not men."

"But I haven't even been to college yet."

Rev. Carlson looked at Peter with a mischievous twinkle in his eyes. "Did your father go to college?"

"Well, no, sir, but—"

"Could he preach?"

"Well, yes, sir, but—"

"Did your stepfather go to college?"

"Well, yes, sir, but—"

"Can he preach?"

"Well, no, sir, but—"

"Well, there you have it!"

A small chuckle came from the area of the dishpile.

"Preaching is a gift from God, son. Either you have it or you don't. I'm not against college, mind you—if it's the right kind. But there are very few of them around. And I've seen the other kind ruin many a good man.

"If you've got the gift, use it. And there's no better time to start using it than the present."

Seeing that things were beginning to take on a more serious tone, Martha Carlson excused herself and left the room.

"But what if I'm not really called to preach?"

"Did you believe God was calling you last Friday when you came forward and surrendered your will to Him?"

"Well, yes, sir, but—"

"Did God change His mind?"

"Well, no, sir, but—"

"Did you?"

The simple question pierced Peter's heart like an arrow. He lowered his eyes to escape Rev. Carlson's intense gaze. Retracing the pattern on the sofa cushion, his mind raced wildly with the events of the past two weeks: his visit to the little rescue mission and decision to preach, his encounters with his stepfather, the fool he'd made of himself in church, his mother—

"I can't!" he cried in anguish, jumping from his seat and crossing to the one little window that faced the narrow street in front of the mission.

He wished Rev. Carlson would just leave him alone. Hadn't he been through enough? If only he could escape from it all—start over—maybe go someplace where nobody knew him.

"Why, son?"

Without replying, Peter pressed his face against the window and looked down at the scene below. There was a woman passing by, aged beyond her years by a life of wickedness and sin. Two men stood outside of the tavern across the street in the middle of a drunken brawl. A little child sat on a doorstep crying. All of them seemed to be tugging at his heart. All of humanity seemed to cry out to him—all of them—lost!

Peter closed his eyes against the scene, trying to block out the Spirit's conviction that seemed to be pulling him apart.

"I just can't, sir."

Peter felt a strong arm across his shoulders. "You're angry at God, aren't you, son?" John Carlson spoke softly now. "You don't understand why He allowed all of this to happen to you: why your father had to be killed, why your mother had to marry Rev. Mooring, why your stepfather hates you so much, even why He had to call *you* to preach."

Peter's eyes stung.

"Am I right, son?"

"Yes, sir," Peter replied quietly.

"I've been there too, Peter. Oftentimes a man goes through a real personal struggle right after he has yielded himself completely to the Lord. Sometimes it's the devil trying to snatch away the precious seed that's been planted in his heart. Sometimes it's the Lord testing him, trying to see what he's made of, and if he really meant it when he said he'd serve Him at any cost. Whatever the case, a man needs to settle it. He can't go on in resentment and bitterness towards God. It's not until we willingly submit ourselves to the good and bad He allows to come into our life that we finally find peace."

Rev. Carlson quietly left the room. Peter stood silently, clenching and unclenching his fists, then dropped to his knees.

A few minutes later, Rev. Carlson answered the soft knock on the bedroom door.

"I'll do it, sir."

Chapter 8

The next few days were full of activity. Rev. Carlson held services at the little mission church on Friday and Saturday nights as well as Sunday morning and evening. His days were composed mostly of ministering to those who stepped inside: curious passersby, wondering how a church managed to get stuck in the middle of Tavern Street; drunken bums looking for a handout; dirty, runny-nosed children with sticky fingers hoping for a piece of candy from the good-hearted minister; former slaves making their way northward in search of work; and a very few sin-wrecked souls who were honestly seeking an escape from their miserable condition.

Peter aided Rev. Carlson wherever he was needed: to follow-up a new convert, quiet a crying child while Mrs. Carlson dealt with its mother about the salvation of her soul, run errands, or help take a drunk who lay unconscious in the gutter to the hospital.

Every spare minute, however, was devoted to his sermon. The fire had begun to blaze again on the altar of his heart, overwhelming him with the same zeal and excitement he had experienced the night of his surrender to preach.

As he pored over the Scriptures looking for just the right text, he tried to imagine the kind of sermon his father would have preached if he were there. This must be a perfect sermon; not the perfection of eloquent speech, precise gestures, or tonal quality, but perfection rising out of a pure heart, a burdened heart, a heart captured by the Almighty, controlled by the Holy Spirit—a message spoken with conviction, convicting souls of sin.

Peter read and reread, compared and pondered, yet nothing seemed to take on any semblance of a sermon.

◆　◆　◆

Thursday night was the one night of the week that Rev. Carlson and his wife allowed themselves the luxury of a night off. Ever since they had begun the little mission at the end of the War Between the States, they had traditionally set aside Thursday night, before all the emotionally draining activities of the weekend, to take a buggy ride out into the country—away from the hustle and bustle of city life, away from the dirt and filth of the slums, away from the cares and concerns of the ministry, to spend a quiet evening together.

"Care to come with us, Peter?" asked Mrs. Carlson sweetly as she adjusted her bonnet in the mirror. "You know you are always welcome."

"Thank you, ma'am, but I had better study."

"Come now, Peter," Rev. Carlson piped in, "you've been studying all week long. It would do you good to take a break; then you can get back to your sermon with a fresh outlook."

"Thank you, sir, but I really feel that I ought to study."

"Haven't decided what to preach on yet?" Rev. Carlson asked with a smile.

"No, sir." Peter hung his head. "I guess I'm getting worried. Time is running out."

"Don't you worry, son." John Carlson clapped him good-naturedly on the back. "God will give you the right sermon when He's ready. And He's never late! Maybe it would be good for you to stay here—give you a chance for some peace and quiet for a change, a time to be alone with the Lord for a while instead of having to listen to all of Mrs. Carlson's constant chatter." He grinned at his quiet, shy wife. They all knew who the real culprit was.

Martha Carlson blushed at her husband's teasing. "John," she said demurely.

◆   ◆   ◆

After the Carlsons had gone, Peter sat down at the kitchen table and laid his Bible in front of him, then, resting his head on his folded hands, prayed: "Oh, Lord, You have got to help me! Please, please show me what You want me to preach. You know I have never done anything like this before, and—I'm scared, Lord!"

He looked up and stared absent-mindedly at the wall for a few seconds, then opened his Bible and began thumbing through the New Testament, glancing at the chapter headings as he went. "Let's see," he muttered to himself, "the parable of the mustard seed, John the Baptist beheaded, feeding of the 5000, the disciples' unbelief, Jesus speaks on forgiveness—forgiveness!"

Peter perused the first few verses. "Then came Peter to him and said, 'Lord, how oft shall my brother sin against me, and I forgive him? Till seven times?' Jesus saith unto him, 'I say not unto thee, until seven times, but until seventy times seven.' "

"Seventy times seven," he mused. "Let's see, that's 490 times! That's a lot of forgiveness—and yet it is nothing when compared to the number of times that the Lord has forgiven us."

He read the two verses again.

"That's it!" he thought. "The subject of forgiveness is so vast. Surely it can be developed into a good sermon—and it is exactly what the people around here need to hear!"

Peter began searching the Scriptures now for related verses, jotting down ideas and references as they came to his mind. He had perfect peace that this was the topic the Lord would have him preach about. And yet, a vague feeling of uneasiness settled over him. The more he read, the more intense the apprehension became. He tried to push it into the corner of his mind, but it continued to creep back, each time growing in its intensity.

"What's wrong with me!" he thought aloud. "I know this is what I am to preach, but why this unsettledness?"

He tried blocking it out of his mind once more by concentrating harder on the verses before him. But the more he studied them, the more it seemed as if his heart were being ripped in two.

Finally, in despair, he sank to his knees by the table, clutching his Bible in his hand. "Lord, I can't go on! I must know what is wrong! I want to please You, but I—"

Suddenly something clicked in his mind. He opened his Bible and nervously paged through it again until he came upon the two verses that had so attracted his attention before. "Then came Peter to him and said, 'Lord, how oft shall my brother sin against me, and I forgive him? Till seven times?'

Jesus saith unto him, 'I say not unto thee, until seven times, but until seventy times seven.' "

He moaned. "Oh, Lord, I can't!" He looked up toward the ceiling as if he were gazing straight through it to Heaven's portals. "It's too hard! Ask me to do anything else, Lord, but I can't forgive him!"

◆　◆　◆

The sound of footsteps on the stairs brought Peter to his feet. Quickly, he went over to the table and began gathering his notes together.

The door opened.

"Well, Peter, how was your evening?" Rev. Carlson removed his cloak and handed it to his wife.

"Fine, sir," Peter returned, not looking up from his papers.

"Looks like you've been busy."

"Yes, sir."

"Did the Lord give you a sermon?" Rev. Carlson smiled, but Peter didn't notice. He was still gazing absently at the papers in his hand.

"Yes, sir."

Rev. Carlson looked intently at his young charge. Peter continued to stare blankly at his notes, trying to evade those eyes that seemed able to pierce right through him into the depths of his soul.

John Carlson excused himself after a few moments and joined his wife in the bedroom. Relieved, Peter quickly changed into his nightshirt and lay down on the couch for a fitful night's sleep.

Chapter 9

The next morning at breakfast everyone was unusually quiet. Peter stared at his plate, toying with his fork and occasionally poking at his egg. His forehead gathered in worried wrinkles, betraying the turmoil that was taking place in his soul.

The Carlsons exchanged sympathetic, perplexed looks with each other as they tried to pretend they had an appetite. Peter really had become almost a son to them, and it hurt them to see him so unhappy.

Finally, the ordeal of breakfast was over, and Rev. Carlson got out his Bible for family devotions.

"Let's see. We've been reading in Matthew. Yesterday we finished chapter 18, so today we'll begin with chapter 19."

Peter's heart skipped a beat. Not chapter

19! He couldn't bear it. Did Rev. Carlson know about the deep dark secrets of his mind, or was it just a coincidence that these verses were the same ones that had haunted him all night long, or—had God planned it that way? Whatever the case, Peter knew he could not stay to hear the rest.

"May I be excused, sir?" he blurted out abruptly in the middle of verse two.

"Why, yes, I suppose you may." Rev. Carlson seemed startled, but asked no questions.

Peter mumbled a quick "thank you" and headed out the door.

"Oh, John," Martha Carlson grasped her husband's hand helplessly, "what do you suppose is wrong?"

"I don't know, Martha, but I have a feeling it's something that only he and the Lord can settle."

◆　◆　◆

The cool morning air felt good against Peter's face. A sudden gust of wind rustled his hair and slightly stung his cheeks, making him feel invigorated. It seemed more like fall weather than summer, and Peter thrilled to it. For a moment he felt like a carefree boy sailing a kite as he ran along the edge of a rippling brook.

A drunk staggered against him, "Why don'cha watch where yer goin', kid!" he said as he reeled off down the broken sidewalk. Peter watched him in disgust until he disappeared from view. He hated the drunk, his stepfather, and everyone else who made the world so miserable.

"Forgiveness," he thought aloud as he resumed his walk. "How can I preach on forgiveness? It takes love to forgive. My father had that kind of love, love for a drunken bum just like that one—and it killed him! Well, I don't!"

The sound of his voice breaking the stillness of the morning startled Peter. He quickly glanced around to see if anyone had heard. Satisfied that he was alone, he slid down on the sidewalk and leaned back against the old abandoned brick warehouse that towered eerily above him. He closed his eyes and sighed.

"There's just too much to forgive, Lord. You don't understand all the things he's done and said to me, and—"

Almost as if a voice from Heaven were speaking to his heart, the words of Christ resounded in his ears. "Father, forgive them, for they know not what they do." Visions of a bleeding, suffering Savior lingered in his mind: the torment, the anguish, the shame.

"Oh, Lord," he sobbed aloud. "I have nothing to forgive, not compared to what You have forgiven. Oh, Lord, I need that—I need Your love and Your grace to forgive. I can't preach unless I have it. How can I tell others of Your forgiveness if I refuse to forgive? Dear Jesus, help me in my weakness. Give me the grace not only to forgive and love him, but to ask his forgiveness for what I said that day in church. I know he doesn't know You as Savior, Lord. Please—use me to bring him to Yourself."

A deep peace flooded his soul. Suddenly all the events of the past few weeks fit together. He was sure that this was what the Lord intended—to use the circumstances that had taken place to bring his stepfather to Christ.

With renewed joy and vigor, Peter got up and dusted himself off. He whistled a lively tune to himself as he walked briskly back to the mission.

When he arrived, he found that both Rev. and Mrs. Carlson were gone. There was a note for him tacked on the door.

Dear Peter,
Sally Turner died last night. We have gone to comfort the family. Do not know when we will return. Pray.

Love,
The Carlsons

"Poor old Sally Turner," he thought as he carefully removed the note and walked inside the cozy front room. "She probably drank herself to death in a gutter some-where." He tried to imagine how discouraged and heartbroken the Carlsons must be. They had spent countless hours counseling with Sally and years of prayer and selfless love, yet she just couldn't let go of her bottle and allow Christ to satisfy her needs.

Peter was rather glad, though, that he had the apartment to himself. It would be a whole lot easier this way to do what he knew had to be done. He walked over to the secretary and drew out a piece of paper, then, pen in hand, sat down to his task.

"Oh, Lord, help me to know what to say and how to say it," he prayed as he began writing.

Dear Sir,

I know that I owe you an apology for what I said about you in church. I did not intend to say what I did; however, the truth remains that I did say it. I want you to know that I deeply regret it. If my actions are responsible for your refusal from Harvard, then I ask your forgiveness for that also.

I am willing to make any restitution that you deem necessary, be it apologizing to the church or the men from Harvard.

Please do not think that I am saying this in order to come home, although God knows how much I desire that. I am sincerely sorry for the heartbreak I have caused, and I beg your forgiveness.

Respectfully,
Peter

Peter inspected the letter several times. He was tempted to leave out the part about making restitution, but, believing that it was the right thing to say, and that God would give him the grace to do whatever his stepfather would require, he left it as it was.

"There," he announced to himself triumphantly as he gave the envelope with its important contents an approving pat, "I'll send it to him tonight through Nanna."

Chapter 10

Sunday afternoon came all too soon for Peter. He was both excited and petrified to see how he would do at preaching his first sermon. He was hoping, too, that his mother would be there. The First Church didn't hold services on Sunday nights, and Aunt Kathryn had promised that she would try to sneak Mrs. Mooring out of the house. He was secretly hoping that they wouldn't have to sneak out, that Rev. Mooring, compelled and softened by his letter, would escort them there himself. Although fully aware that the reality of such a hope would be nothing short of a miracle, Peter encouraged his reverie in the fact that his God was the God of miracles. Regardless of the outcome, he was certain that the Holy Spirit was working in his stepfather's heart. It just had to be so. He had prayed so hard, and claimed God's promise that "all things work together for good to them that love Him."

He was sure that his stepfather had seen the letter by now. Nanna had been given strict orders to take it directly to him as soon as she had arrived home Friday night, without peeking at it herself. Peter chuckled to himself as he recalled the response she had given him, her eyes twinkling mischievously. "Why, Peter, I'm shocked that you would think such a thing of me. I'd never think of prying into something that wasn't any of my business!"

It was almost time for the service to begin. Peter and Rev. Carlson took their places in the front. Mrs. Carlson seated herself at the piano bench and began playing some hymns. A few people straggled in. Rev. Carlson was pleased to see Mr. Turner in the audience. Two recent converts entered, chattering pleasantly to each other.

"What a change in their faces from the

first time I saw them," Peter mused. "Then they were haggard and weary; now, they seem to shine." He decided that he really loved mission work. Although it brought with it heartaches all its own, there were occasional rewards, like those reflected in the glowing faces before him, that made the hours of hard work and prayer worthwhile. He wondered how many stars Rev. and Mrs. Carlson would find in their crowns when they reached Heaven's shore.

Martha Carlson was on her last hymn before the start of the service. He knew, because he'd seen her give her husband that special wink she always gave when her repertoire was about to be exhausted and he was to take over.

Peter strained his eyes to see out the front window. Surely his mother and Kathryn would be coming soon. Then he heard carriage wheels approaching. Leaning forward, he anticipated the stop of the carriage bringing his loved ones. Oh, how he longed to see his beloved mother. He could hardly believe it had been three weeks since he had last laid eyes on her.

But the carriage clattered noisily by. Peter tried not to show his disappointment. Rev. Carlson was asking the people to open their hymnbooks to "Amazing Grace." Numbly, Peter turned to the correct page and stood to sing with the small group of about twenty. He tried to encourage himself by telling himself that they were just late, and that any minute he would hear the soft rustle of their long skirts against the rough wooden floor and look into the faces of those he loved so dearly.

◆ ◆ ◆

The time for Peter's sermon came and went. Peter really didn't know how well he had done, although several shook his hand and told him what a wonderful sermon it had been, and one old woman had come to the front for counseling, and was even now sobbing out her story of sin and woe to Mrs. Carlson in the back room. He was too numb. He couldn't remember what he had said, or even how he had managed to get through it. All that he knew was that several times during the message he had had the urge to run away and had to bite his lip to keep the tears from flowing.

When everyone had finally gone, Mrs. Carlson retreated upstairs, giving the excuse that she was very tired. Peter felt certain that the real purpose was to give him and Rev. Carlson a chance to be alone.

The two stood silently for what seemed to Peter to be an eternity.

"That was a fine sermon you preached, son."

"Thank you, sir." Peter hung his head

and stared at the floor.

"I—I know how disappointed you must be, Peter. All is not lost, son. There will be other sermons. Maybe something important came up."

"Maybe."

"You know your mother would have been here if it were at all possible."

"I know, sir. That's what I can't understand. Surely after he read the letter—"

"Letter?"

He hadn't meant to tell anyone, but now that it was revealed, Peter found himself relating the whole story to the sympathetic minister.

"I just don't understand, sir. I was so sure that the Lord would use that letter to begin working on his heart."

"Perhaps that's your answer, Peter."

"Sir?"

"That the Lord would use your letter to *begin* working on your stepfather's heart. You see, Peter, God's timing is not the same as ours. With Him, one day is as a thousand years, and a thousand years as one day."

"But why would that hinder mother and Nanna from coming? Certainly the letter couldn't have made him angrier. And, even if it did, I mentioned nothing about their coming, or even that I was going to preach. How could he have known? I'm sure neither one of them would have let it slip."

"We're just guessing that he kept them from coming. Chances are, he had nothing at all to do with it. Maybe they're ill."

Peter shook his head. "I don't think so, sir. I don't think they would have allowed sickness to interfere with their coming, not unless it was—serious."

Rev. Carlson placed a strong hand on Peter's shoulder. "Please don't let it worry you, son."

◆　◆　◆

It was easy to say, "don't let it worry you," but hard to live. Although Peter tried and tried to forget the incident—tried to pass it off as just a simple misunderstanding, deep down, he couldn't help worrying about it. Time after time he found himself having to ask the Lord's forgiveness for the hateful, resentful thoughts toward his stepfather that swept over him, eating away at the very core of his being.

His mind conjured up reason after reason as to why his mother and Kathryn had not been there to hear him preach. If one of them were truly sick, he wanted to go and comfort them, yet he was helpless; if something had happened to them on the way, he wanted to know, but all lines of communication had been cut off; if Rev. Mooring had—there it was again! No matter how hard he endeavored to think to the contrary, somehow he would return to the thought that his stepfather was at the root of it, and that somehow, the letter he had so carefully and sincerely written had been used against him.

"Why, Lord?" he questioned time and again. "Why would You allow this to happen? I know I did the right thing by writing that letter. I was so sure that everything was going to work out so perfectly. I had my hopes built so high, Lord. How could You allow it? How could I have been so disillusioned? It isn't fair," his heart cried out. "It isn't fair!"

Just when he felt as if he would be overcome with despair, a ray of hope would shine through the gloom. Maybe Kathryn hadn't understood what Sunday he'd meant. Maybe next Sunday night they would enter the little mission, expecting to hear him preach, and all his dismal thoughts would prove to have been only futile efforts at self-torture.

Surely the Lord would not let him down. Not after he had given himself so completely to His will. God had promised that "all things would work together for good." He would not be defeated by figments of his imagination. He would claim that promise, cling to that promise, for all it was worth.

But the seasons of victory and self-encouragement were short-lived. Soon, he would find himself plunging headlong into the former turmoil and begin the cycle again.

Rev. and Mrs. Carlson could not help but take notice of the boy's sudden changes of mood. One minute he would be whistling a hymn as he went about his chores or helped them on an errand of mercy. The next, he would seem to sink into a faraway world of his own—a world of trouble, of sorrow and pain.

When two more weeks passed without any word from the parsonage on Elm Street, Peter sank into a constant state of depression. He became short-tempered, irritable, and restless.

"Peter," Rev. Carlson remarked one bright, sunny morning, "I've decided to give you the day off. I want you to go somewhere, do something just for the fun of it."

"Such as?"

"Such as going to the Centennial Exhibition! I've heard great things about it. Seems they have some pretty fascinating machines on display there that they say are really going to change the way we live."

"Are you and Mrs. Carlson going?" he asked uninterestedly.

"Not today. You need time to be alone, for a whole day, just to do as you please."

"What you're really trying to say is that you couldn't stand to be around me for another day."

"Now, son, I didn't say that or imply it."

"It doesn't matter, sir. I know I've been miserable to be around. If I could, I'd get away from myself, but I'm stuck."

"It was just a suggestion, Peter. I thought it might help." The graying man turned quietly away.

"Sir. I—I'm sorry. The last thing on earth I want to do is to hurt you and Mrs. Carlson. You've been so good to me and I—well, I'm sorry for what I just said."

"It's all right, son. Mrs. Carlson and I feel so helpless standing by just watching you suffer. I've considered going to see your stepfather myself. I thought maybe he'd listen to me."

"No! Please, sir. You don't know what he's like. I wouldn't dare ask it of you. Besides, it might only make things worse. I've thought several times of going back myself, but I know it would do no good."

"We are praying for you, son. God will answer. We must trust Him. In the meantime, why don't you take the day off and relax—get your mind off things for a day. It will do you good."

"I suppose you're right, sir. I'll do it. I've been rather hoping I could see the Exhibition before it closes."

"Here, Peter, take this." Rev. Carlson pressed a few coins into his hand. "I know it isn't much, but perhaps you'll see something there that you'd like."

Peter looked at the silver coins in his hand and shook his head. "Thank you, sir, but I can't take your money. You and Mrs. Carlson have so little to begin with. I should be paying you. I would be, if—"

Peter tried to give the money back, but Rev. Carlson only pressed it back into his hand again. "You deserve it, son. You've helped us so much, and you'll never know what your being here has done for me and the Missus. Her one desire that was never fulfilled was to have a child. You can't begin to imagine how her mother-heart has thrilled to your being here.   Please, take it, for her sake."

"I will, sir. Thank you."

Chapter 11

Rev. Carlson had said that Peter could use the buggy, and now he was thoroughly enjoying a leisurely jaunt past the slum district and out onto Park Avenue, lined on either side with huge maple trees, their leafy branches casting dancing shadows on the wide cobblestone street. The air seemed so much cleaner here. Peter drank in every stately house and garden that had been such a part of the last ten years of his life. Yet they seemed almost a part of a dream, a page from a book, an episode of faraway and long ago.

Ahead of him lay Elm Street, the First Church, the parsonage, his mother. As he neared the corner, his heart began to thump wildly, his throat tightened. He dared himself to drive past the parsonage, perhaps to even knock on the back door and find Nanna there to greet him with open arms. Or better yet, he would glance up at a bedroom window—his bedroom—and find his mother, her golden hair tossing in the wind, waving out at him, smiling, beckoning him to "come home."

He pulled the reins tightly to the right. A wave of dizziness surged over him. He couldn't do it. His mother would not see him, Kathryn would not be there. Instead, his stepfather would be waiting for him. Waiting to—

Peter snapped the reins again, and the horse trotted forward. Perhaps he would have the courage to go by after he'd been to the Exhibition, but not now.

When Peter arrived at the Exhibition grounds, he found it crawling with people. This was the biggest event of the Centennial in the whole country. People from all over the nation, as well as 50 foreign countries, had come to view in awe the miracles of modern man's inventive mind.

All around him were buildings, huge buildings covering hundreds of acres. Peter thought it should take an entire week for one to see the whole exhibit, and he hardly knew where to begin.

In the first building he discovered table after table of handcrafted items: clocks, furniture, jewelry, silverware. Glassblowers heated thin pipes of glass and transformed them into beautiful multicolored vases, pitchers, and glasses before the eyes of the amazed onlookers. Weavers demonstrated their talents on huge wooden looms, while artists cajoled mothers and fathers into allowing them to paint a portrait of their "darling children." Knitting, crocheting, tatting, embroidery, and needlework of every description embellished each nook and cranny.

The next building contained fabulous new machines: the typewriter, an invention that Peter felt would be sure to decrease valuable time in correspondence for busy people such as Rev. Carlson. He marveled how anyone could ever learn how to use it though, since the letters were so jumbled up. The telephone—who would have thought that one day people could actually talk to each other from their homes? The telegraph had seemed a fantastic invention, and surely

Thomas Edison's duplex telegraph that could send two messages over the same wire at the same time was next to miraculous. Peter doubted that it would ever be supplanted by the telephone—there would have to be wires running everywhere. Besides, one couldn't send messages as far on a telephone as over a telegraph. No, he supposed it would be quite a while before that new-fangled invention would be put to practical use.

The next building was much smaller than the first two, containing booths filled with wonderful souvenirs of the momentous occasion and concession stands with popcorn balls, fudge, and ice cream. He decided to try some Old Philadelphia ice cream. The company had just recently opened, and he'd heard that they had the best ice cream in the world. After he tasted it, he was sure they must be right.

The fourth building contained more inventions: a self-binding reaper, Westinghouse air brakes, and a refrigerator car.

Peter was so fascinated by all the new sights and sounds around him that he had completely forgotten his troubles. Rev. Carlson had been right. This was just what he had needed.

As he left the fourth building, he took a deep breath of the fragrant fresh air. He laughed at a nearby photographer who was trying desperately to get a child who was posing for a picture to stop crying. The child was offered toys and candy, made faces at, tickled, but alas, nothing worked, and the disheartened parents whisked him off the little bench and took him home, scolding as they went, the little tyke still bawling his protest.

Ahead of Peter was a building that seemed so crowded with people he just had to get a glimpse of what was inside. Above the door, a huge sign coaxed the multitudes to come and see "The Corliss Steam Engine."

"That I'd like to see," he thought as he began wedging his way in with the crowd. Everyone was pushing and shoving, as if they were afraid the engine would disappear before they had a chance to view it. Someone behind Peter accidentally bumped into him, causing him to fall against the man in front of him.

"Excuse me, sir," Peter said politely.

The man turned around and looked at him with a smile that quickly faded into a sneer. Peter's heart seemed to stop beating.

"Well, well, well," said the stately gentleman, "if it isn't the prodigal son!"

Peter didn't answer. He was too stunned.

"How are things in the slums, boy?"

Peter winced at the insult. "Fine, sir," he replied meekly. He glanced around to see who was listening. Several heads were turned their way. If only he could get away, but the people were packaged together so tightly that they were being jostled along with the crowd without having to make any effort of their own to move.

"Aren't you going to ask me if I got your letter?"

Peter didn't answer.

"I beg your forgiveness," he quoted sarcastically. "I wouldn't forgive you for what you did to me if you came crawling on your knees, boy!"

Peter swallowed hard. He wished his stepfather would lower his voice.

"I—I'm sorry you feel that way, sir."

"I imagine you are, boy! By the way, have you been wondering why your mother and Kathryn didn't come to hear you preach your first sermon? Don't look so shocked, boy! I know all about it. And do you know who told me?" He was gloating at Peter triumphantly, as if he'd just begun to win a war he was losing.

"No, sir."

"You did!"

Peter stood in stunned silence. He didn't know what to say. He didn't see how he possibly could have tipped him off since his letter mentioned nothing.

"You thought you were so smart writing that letter. You probably thought I'd come begging you to come home. Well, you needn't ever worry about that, boy, because it will never happen!"

They were nearing the door now. Peter secretly hoped he could lose his stepfather once they were inside.

"Well?" the big man bellowed. "Don't you want to hear how I discovered your little scheme?"

"Yes, sir."

"You thought you had everything polished over, but you made two mistakes, boy—two stupid mistakes!"

Peter winced again. He could feel the eyes around them taking in the scene they were making just as he had the little boy who was having his picture taken.

"Want to know what stupid mistakes you made, boy?" Peter knew that his stepfather was purposely goading him, trying to make each word hurt as much as possible, trying to make him feel small and insignificant. It had always been that way. And his stepfather had always managed to achieve the desired results, just as he was now.

"Yes, sir."

"You said you were sorry I didn't get the job at Harvard. I began wondering how you knew I hadn't received the position. I also wondered how Kathryn happened to come upon the letter, since it had no address or stamp. So I started asking questions."

Peter shifted his eyes to the ground.

"Aunt Kathryn may be a little sneaky, but she won't lie. I discovered that she had been to see you. And I also found out that your mother and she were planning to come hear their darling Peter preach. Huh! As if a boy could stand up and speak anything noteworthy!"

Each word was like a slap across his face. Peter bit his lip to keep from saying anything he would later regret, and prayed for grace. They were inside now, and Peter quickened his pace.

"I'm not finished with you yet, boy!"

Again Peter felt the stares around him. He wondered how his stepfather could be so oblivious to them. He had no choice but to meekly stay and take the indignities being hurled at him.

"Kathryn won't be coming to see you anymore."

Peter closed his eyes to try and block out what he knew was sure to follow.

"And neither will your mother!"

Reaching for the wrought iron railing that separated the crowds from the inventions, Peter leaned his full weight against it. His legs seemed to buckle under him. He felt dizzy, weak.

"Nor will you receive any letters or money from them. I have forbidden them to have any further contact with you!"

"Why, sir?" Peter questioned brokenly,

unbidden tears surfacing in his eyes. He could not, would not allow himself to cry in front of his stepfather. "I asked your forgiveness. What more do you want me to do?"

"I want you to stay out of my life! Go back to the slums where you belong! I hate you, boy! Do you understand? I hate you! If I never laid eyes on you again it would be too soon!"

The words twisted and turned in Peter's heart like a knife. The tears stung at his eyes. He must control himself! He would not give the Rev. Mooring the pleasure of knowing just how much he was hurting.

"Are you finished, sir?"

"No! There's just one more thing I want you to know. If I ever find any more letters from you to anyone in my house, I'll burn them! And if you ever set foot on my property, I'll have you arrested for trespassing! Do you understand?"

Peter tightened his grip on the railing. For a moment, the floor and ceiling became one, swirling madly around him. He took a deep breath. How he wanted to hate the man in front of him—but he couldn't. He was too tired, too crushed, too broken.

"I understand, sir."

Chapter 12

Peter cracked the whip above the horse's head. All the pent-up feelings and frustrations of the past few weeks combined with the abuses he had just endured seemed as if they would rise up and strangle him. There was a painful gnawing in the pit of his stomach. His head swam. His eyes stung. His heart ached.

Elm Street. The sign quietly mocked him as it urged him to ride down her street and visit her inhabitants: his mother—held like a prisoner in her own house, Kathryn—torn between her love for Peter and her obligation to her brother's son, James—the quiet butler who had always somehow managed to stay out of the family quarrels, and Rev. Mooring—the man who hated him.

Peter cracked the whip once more and the horse quickened her gait. He had dared himself earlier that day to ride down that street and up to the stately columns that adorned the front of the colonial mansion that had been his home. His home—now it was a forbidden land.

He challenged himself now to go through

with his dare. He imagined himself being dragged off the immaculate grounds by two burly policemen. "What would his parishoners think of their Reverend after a scene like that?" he thought. "Probably he would manage to weasel out of it somehow and cast the blame back on his 'prodigal son.'" Peter wondered what it would be like to be in jail. Would he ever get out? Would his stepfather pay off the judge and have him committed for life?

A shudder swept over him, sending chills down his back. He thought he would not mind risking it if it were not for the sake of his mother. But he must think of her—he could not bear to cause her any more suffering, and it grieved him to think of the suffering she had already gone through and was even at this moment enduring.

His mother—would he, in truth, never see her again?

Somehow it all seemed like a nightmare—an incredible nightmare that couldn't possibly be true. Soon he would awaken and find himself back in the little cottage playing by the fireside while his father whittled a new toy for him, and his mother, rocking away in her favorite chair, sang them both a song, the knitting needles clicking rapidly along in rhythm.

But it wasn't a nightmare. Bizarre as it all seemed, it was real, and he would never be able to awaken from it.

The buggy rounded the corner into the slum district. What a contrast to the elegant setting he had just come from. Instead of the beautiful mansions and broad avenues lined with stately trees, there were row upon row of small brick and wooden shanties, crowded together on dirty alleyways, barren of all greenery. The air smelled of whiskey and disease. Dirty children knelt on the narrow curb playing jacks, while men and women of ill repute staggered in and out of taverns and brothels. Was this where he belonged? Would he be destined to spend the rest of his life in such surroundings?

It had been a welcome relief from the pomp and circumstance of high society—but only on a temporary basis. Surely the Lord didn't expect him to waste away the rest of his life in this—this God-forsaken place.

If only he had kept his mouth shut. He would probably have been enrolled in Harvard by now. His stepfather would have been one of the noted faculty. He might have graduated with honors—beloved and adored by all. Perhaps he would have become a doctor or lawyer. Instead, he had thrown his life away for this!

He pulled the reins to the left and the horse trotted briskly onto Tavern Street. Ahead of him, to the right, lay the mission.

He tethered the horse outside and

quietly entered the narrow building, breathing a sigh of relief that no one was there. He scrutinized the little room that served as a chapel: the unfinished floor, broken-down piano, and rough benches. He walked to the little back room that had served as overnight lodging for many a drunken bum. "More like a prison cell," he thought.

Peter trudged wearily up the rickety, creaking stairs to the Carlson's apartment. He listened in at the keyhole before entering. Not a sound. Perhaps he would not have to face them—at least for a while.

Convinced that no one was home, he opened the door and walked in.

"That you, John?" Mrs. Carlson appeared in the bedroom doorway, her arms full of clean sheets. "Oh, Peter, you're home early."

For a moment Peter saw his mother standing there in her place: the simple calico dress, starched white apron, loving smile—just as a mother should look. He turned away quickly and bit down on his lip.

"Did you enjoy the Exhibition?"

"Yes, ma'am. It—it was wonderful." He tried his best to sound convincing. If only he didn't have to look at her again—maybe she wouldn't be able to tell that his soul was in agony.

At any other time, Martha Carlson probably would have detected the quaver in his voice, but she was too preoccupied now to notice.

"You'll have to tell us all about it tonight, after John comes home with our new guest."

"Guest?" he repeated dully. What he didn't need right now were more people gawking at him in his misery.

"Yes. I'm going to have two children now!" She plumped the pillows on the couch, Peter wondered how anyone in the world could be so happy while someone else was so sad. All of her dreams were being fulfilled while his were being shattered.

"A girl and a boy," she continued brightly. "I always wanted a girl and a boy." She sighed contentedly. "Oh, I hope you don't mind sleeping in the room downstairs. It might not be safe for Amy."

Amy—so that was the name of the intruder who was to steal away from him the last little semblance of a home.

"We didn't think you would mind. It's really not safe for a girl down there, since drunks sometimes break in, but we thought you could handle it."

Knowing his eyes would betray him, Peter kept his face turned away from her and said nothing.

"You don't mind, do you?"

"No, ma'am. Of course not."

Martha Carlson was relieved. She wouldn't think of doing anything to hurt the homeless lad that had become so much a part of their family. She began setting the supper plates on the table.

"Mrs. Carlson?" Peter tried to keep his voice from shaking.

"Yes?"

"Would you—would you mind if I just went down to my room now?"

"Not at all, Peter. If you'd like to rest before dinner, the bed's already made up."

"I—I don't think I'll be at dinner tonight, ma'am."

"Oh?" Martha Carlson stopped laying out the silverware and looked at him. Although his back was turned towards her, she noticed his hand go up to his face and quickly brush something away from his eyes.

"Peter? What is it? Are—are you all right?" She laid a gentle hand on his arm.

"Yes, ma'am," he answered, choking back the tears. "I—I'm fine. I'd just like to be left alone tonight if I may."

"Of course."

As if in a daze, Peter stumbled out the door and down the stairs to the little back room. He thrust himself on the little cot, and the once forbidden tears now fell in torrents on the white patched pillow case. Peter buried his head in the little pillow and allowed the tears to flow freely. "All alone," he mused pensively, "in my prison cell."

Chapter 13

The next morning Peter arose with a pounding headache and a gnawing pain in his stomach. The fresh aroma of bacon and eggs, wafting downward from the little kitchen above, taunted and beckoned him at the same time.

He rubbed his blood-shot eyes and ran his fingers back through his tousled hair. The night had been a miserable one with only short spurts of sleep interspersed with memories of the past, visions of his mother, and re-enactments of the chance encounter with his stepfather.

Wearily, he got up and began dressing. He discovered that Mrs. Carlson had put all of his clothes, few as they were, in the small pine chest that stood in the corner of his "cell."

"Guess what's-her-name is going to be a permanent fixture around here," he grumbled to himself.

Peter sank against the chest and leaned his elbows on the top. Resting his head in his hands, he gave a long, pitiful sigh. Never before had he experienced such loneliness. When he'd had to leave his mother, the Carlsons had been there to replace the vacuum in his soul. Now they had been taken from him—snatched away by that—girl.

A portion of a verse he'd once read flashed through his mind. "When my mother and father forsake me, then the Lord will take me up."

"Oh, Lord," he cried brokenly, "take me up. Please, take me up. I can't bear any more rejection."

Peter heard movement above him and knew that they must soon be ready for breakfast. How he wished he did not have to face them, but the smell of food increased the gnawing in his stomach, coaxing him on. He paused at the door, and with heavy eyes once again perused his "cell"—dingy white ceiling, gray walls, plain patched sheets, and rough wooden floor. Every corner and shadow seemed to call jeeringly out at him— "Forsaken, forsaken—forsaken!"

◆　　◆　　◆

There was a knock on the door.

"Hmm, wonder who that could be at this hour in the morning?" Rev. Carlson remarked casually as he opened the door.

"Why, Peter!" exclaimed Mrs. Carlson, breaking an egg into the frying pan. "You don't need to knock! This is your home!"

Peter only grunted in reply and took his place at the table. He noticed that it was set for four. No doubt he would soon have the pleasure of meeting "the intruder."

"Amy will be out in a minute. We're eager for you to meet her," chattered Mrs. Carlson excitedly.

"And I thought we were eager for her to meet you," chuckled Rev. Carlson, folding his arms sternly and looking askance at Peter's disheveled appearance.

Noticing that Peter did not look up nor smile, Rev. Carlson quickly changed the subject.

"Ah, how did you find the Exhibition to be, son?"

"Fine, sir," Peter remarked briskly.

Mrs. Carlson gave her husband a despairing look, and not knowing what other subject to switch to, the good Reverend said no more.

Presently, the door to the bedroom opened softly. Peter knew that "she" was standing there, probably taking in the shabby outcast with one disparaging glance. He could feel all eyes glued upon him, yet he did not raise his eyes. He was being pulled apart; wishing that he could either run away, the possibility of which he had mulled over in his mind many times during the previous restless night, or that someone would soon introduce the stranger so he could have an excuse to look up and not feel so awkward.

"Peter," Rev. Carlson broke into the excruciating silence, "I'd like you to meet Amy Richardson, a very dear friend of ours."

Peter rose politely, still not daring to look up, and took the soft hand which had been extended to him.

"I'm very pleased to meet you, sir. The Carlsons have told me so much about you. All good, I assure you."

There was a lilt and smile to the little girl voice that compelled Peter to look up into the face of his rival.

She was beautiful! Long, dark, glossy hair—laughing brown eyes half hidden by thick, dark lashes—cute up-turned nose—small mouth. She was a petite little lady dressed in simple blue gingham, yet her smile and bearing made her appear almost regal.

"I—I'm pleased to meet you, ma'am." Peter self-consciously felt his unshaven face. What a sight he must be! He caught a twinkle in Rev. Carlson's eyes and what looked to be a slight smile spreading across his face that almost caused Peter to laugh in spite of himself.

Suddenly, he realized he had never let go of the newcomer's hand. Embarrassed, he dropped it abruptly and stared at the floor as the crimson rose to his cheeks.

Rev. Carlson managed to stifle a chuckle

as the four sat down to breakfast.

"Dear Lord," he began, "how we thank Thee for Thy provisions; for health, and strength, and love—for these two fine young people that we have the pleasure of sharing our home with. Bless them both, Lord, and meet their every need. Bless now this food to our bodies and us to Thy service. In Jesus' precious and holy name, Amen."

Peter said little during the meal, though his heart was nearly bursting to find out more about the pretty stranger sitting next to him. Somehow he wanted to pour out his heart to her; somehow he felt that she would understand, that she would care. Yet, he dare not let himself think like that. She wouldn't care about him. Why should she? No one else did. No, he would go through with his plan to talk to Rev. Carlson after breakfast. He had made up his mind. He would leave and go somewhere far away where no one knew him—perhaps out West—to start life over again. He would not allow himself to be hurt again by those he had come to love and trust.

After breakfast, Martha and Amy began gathering up the dirty dishes to be washed. John Carlson took his place in his favorite stuffed chair and began reading his Bible.

"Sir," Peter spoke softly so as not to be heard by the two women.

"Yes, son?" Rev. Carlson looked up from his Bible and gazed compassionately into the eyes of the young boy he truly had grown to love as a son.

Peter could see those eyes did not speak of rejection. For a moment, he wavered in his decision, but only for a moment. He must get away! How could he have peace being so close, yet so far, from the dearest person in life to him?

"Could I talk to you for a minute, sir? Alone."

Rev. Carlson nodded sympathetically, and the two crept down the rickety staircase to the little back room.

Chapter 14

Once they had entered the back room, Peter walked directly over to the tiny slit of a window, parted the curtains, and stared blankly at the tumbled-down stable directly behind the chapel. He kept his back toward Rev. Carlson, not wanting to have to look him in the eyes. What he had to say was going to be hard enough as it was.

"Care to sit down, Peter?" asked Rev. Carlson as he lowered himself onto the cot.

"No, thank you, sir. I'd rather stand."

There was a long, pained silence. Peter tried to begin several times, but the words seemed to catch in his throat. He didn't know where to begin nor how to say what needed to be said. He was certain that Rev. Carlson would not understand.

"Peter, I know something is troubling you, son. It will be a lot easier for both of us if we can talk about it," Rev. Carlson spoke gently.

"I—I know, sir. It's just that I—don't know how to say it." Peter continued to stare blankly out the window.

"Just say what's on your heart, son."

Peter nervously clenched and unclenched his fists. He felt weak and shaky.

"I—I'm leaving, sir."

There was no sound from the old man. The silence was almost unbearable for Peter. He knew his words had hurt deeply, but they were out now and could not be retracted. Someday Rev. Carlson would understand that it was for the best, that it had to be done. He just had to get away, to start life over, somewhere where he was needed, wanted, loved.

"Leaving?" Rev. Carlson's voice shook.

"Yes, sir."

"Are you going home?"

"No, sir."

"Then—where?"

"I—I don't know."

Another period of silence followed. Peter thought he could hear the Reverend sniff back tears. He wanted both to comfort him and to run away at the same time, but he kept his back toward the old man and wondered how he could stand to hurt this one who had been so much like a father to him for the past two months. He tried to make himself remember the feelings of rejection and loneliness he had felt the night before, trying to convince himself that he was doing the right thing.

"Why?"

The word echoed and re-echoed in Peter's ears. It was the same question he had asked his stepfather the day before, the same question he had been asking the Lord—"Why?"

"I have to get away, sir, where nobody knows me."

"Haven't we been good to you, Peter?"

Peter took a deep breath.

"Yes, of course you have."

"Then why?" His voice was earnest and broken. "If we've done anything—"

"It's not really because of you, sir."

"Then what is it, son?"

"I—I saw my stepfather yesterday."

"You went home?"

"No, sir—at the Exhibition."

"I'm sorry, Peter. I was the one who told

you to go. Of course, I had no way of knowing."

"I know, sir. I'm not blaming you for that. I really did enjoy the Exhibition. You were right, it was good for me—until I saw him. I literally bumped right into him!"

"Did he say anything?"

"Yes, sir, he said plenty. He called me the prodigal son, laughed my letter to scorn, told me he hated me, and—" Peter leaned his arm against the wall and buried his head in it.

"Go on, son." Rev. Carlson walked over to Peter and placed his big hands gently on the boy's shoulders.

"He said I would never see Nanna—or my mother again!"

There was another long silence, broken only by an occasional stifled sob. Rev. Carlson could think of nothing else to do but pray.

Peter regained his composure and continued. "He said if I ever sent any more letters he'd burn them! And if I ever tried to come home he'd have me arrested for trespassing!"

Peter felt the old resentment and bitterness toward his stepfather springing up in his heart like weeds, choking the forgiveness that had been there.

"And that's why you want to leave?"

"Partly."

"And the other part?"

"I—I can't tell you, sir."

"Why?"

"Because—you'll think me ungrateful—and childish."

"Try me, Peter."

Peter turned around and faced Rev. Carlson for the first time since they had begun their discussion.

"I came home as soon as I could get away from my stepfather, expecting to find sympathy and love—"

"And instead you thought that someone had taken your place. Is that it?"

Peter hung his head. "Yes, sir. Silly isn't it?"

"No, Peter, I don't think it's silly. But, I must confess, that it hurts that you would doubt our love for you, that you would think we would forsake you." Rev. Carlson sank back down on the little cot.

"The last thing in the world I want to do is to hurt you, sir. Perhaps I'll feel differently in a few days. It's just that right now I feel as if I'm being torn apart inside. I guess I don't know how I feel."

"That may be why the good Lord told us to 'walk by faith' instead of sight. Our emotions can play so many tricks on us. Peter, why don't you sit down here for a few minutes and let me tell you a little bit about Amy. I think it will help you to understand about yesterday."

"Please don't misunderstand, sir. I have nothing against Amy."

"Oh, I know that! In fact, judging from your short introduction to her this morning, I would say that your feelings were quite the opposite!"

There was a merry twinkle in the old man's eyes and a wry smile playing at the corner of his lips.

Peter blushed as he sat down beside the minister. "Was it that obvious?"

"Well, I guess!" came the spirited reply.

"I hope I didn't offend her."

"Offend her! I should think not! I was watching her, Peter, and I'd say she was rather pleased to make your acquaintance, even if you did look a bit like a bum." Rev. Carlson cackled to himself.

Peter self-consciously felt his unshaven face once more, then ran his fingers through his uncombed hair as he glanced at himself critically in the little cracked mirror. "I guess I am quite a sight," he laughed.

The more he looked at himself, the more he laughed, and the more he laughed, the more Rev. Carlson laughed, until soon the two were almost in hysterics.

◆　　◆　　◆

Hearing the merriment downstairs and deciding that the worst was over, Mrs. Carlson and Amy returned to their task of dishwashing.

"It sounds to me as though everything is going to be all right," Amy remarked cheerfully.

"Yes—you don't know how good it is to hear that boy laugh, Amy. Lord knows how much he's been through the past two months." Then, noticing the tears that were forming in the young girl's eyes, she added, "and you, dear, have you been able to have a good cry yet?"

"No, Mama Carlson." She struggled to hold back the tears. "I've wanted to cry so much, really cry. But I was in such a state of shock at first and then surrounded only by strangers. Oh, Mama Carlson, hold me tight!"

They were the words she'd always said as a little girl whenever her family had come for a visit. Now, at sixteen, they still seemed appropriate as Amy fell into the loving strong arms of her dear friend and wept unashamedly.

◆　◆　◆

"What a selfish, low-down brat I am!" Peter stated emphatically when Rev. Carlson had finished his story.

"No, you're not, son."

"Yes, I am! Here I am feeling sorry for myself, as if I'm the only one in the world who has any problems. Sometimes I wonder how

85

you and Mrs. Carlson ever put up with me."

"It's not hard, son. You're just human like the rest of us."

"Sometimes I think maybe I'm too human. How can the Lord use me to preach the gospel to others when I'm so weak?"

"If I'm not mistaken, there's a verse in Scripture that says, 'His strength is made perfect in weakness.' If you felt you could do everything on your own, Peter, you wouldn't see your need of Him. God uses the weak things of this world to confound the mighty."

"Well, He certainly has a usable tool in me."

"I think so. But is it a willing tool?"

Peter met the Reverend's deep gaze. "Yes, sir. I haven't forgotten what He's called me to do, and I haven't forsaken it either ... thanks to you."

"Peter, I'm just another one of His weak tools made strong by His power. Agree?"

"Yes, sir." The two clasped hands warmly, then rose to leave.

"There's just one thing that bothers me yet, sir."

"Oh?"

"I—I hope Amy doesn't know of my feelings."

"Which ones?"

Peter blushed again. "You know what I mean, sir—about this morning."

"No, Peter I don't think she surmises a

thing. As I see it, the only One you need to settle things with is the Lord."

"I will, sir."

"Well, I'll go upstairs now. My stomach is telling me it's almost time for lunch, though it seems as if we just finished breakfast. Oh, well. You will join us for lunch, won't you, Peter?"

"Yes, sir."

"Good. Oh, and—ah—do you think you could fix yourself up a little this time before you come?" He winked mischievously.

"Yes, sir!"

Chapter 15

The weeks turned into months at the little mission as things fell into more of a routine.

Elm Street and the parsonage seemed almost as distant and blurred a memory to Peter as those of his father.

Amy had proved to be not only a great help to the Carlsons, but a delight to all those who attended the little mission. Her rich, clear, soprano voice had attracted many newcomers to the services, and several people had been saved as a result.

Peter especially loved to watch her as she sang, her face radiating the love and compassion of God, although at times, when their eyes met, he was afraid of betraying the deep yearnings of his heart that grew stronger with every day.

At other times, he would secretly admire her as she went about her daily tasks at the mission, cleaning, baking, or mending. Rev. Carlson would sometimes give him a knowing look or wink and begin to chuckle, at which point Peter would blush terribly and hope that Rev. Carlson would not burst into laughter or blurt out his secret.

Though Peter longed to tell Amy of his feelings for her, his shyness would not permit him to say more than the casual words general conversation would allow, and each day, as his love for her grew stronger, even those words decreased.

Rev. Carlson, being a tremendous matchmaker at heart, was constantly trying to find ways to encourage their friendship since Amy had also proved to be quite shy. Several times, he and Mrs. Carlson left the dinner table early, leaving the two to strike up a conversation, but it was always to no avail.

One Thursday, he had suggested that the two of them take the buggy and go for a ride instead of he and Mrs. Carlson going, but both Peter and Amy had quickly come up with an excuse as to why they could not possibly go.

◆　　◆　　◆

"John," Mrs. Carlson said sternly on one of their buggy trips, "you really ought to leave those two alone."

"Why? It's fun!" His eyes twinkled merrily. "Besides, how are they ever going to get married if they won't even talk to each other?"

"Married? Who says they want to get married?"

"I do. I can tell."

"How?"

"Oh, I just can."

"John Carlson, you're impossible!"

"Now, just think, Martha. Wouldn't it be just like the Lord to bring them both to our place, at the same time mind you, so they could meet each other and get married?"

"Meet each other, yes. Get married— why John, they've only known each other for two months."

"And how long did we know each other before we knew we were to be husband and wife?"

"Well, about—two months."

"Ah, you see?"

"But, John. It doesn't work that way for

89

everybody."

"I know, I know. But somehow I have a feeling that it will in this case; that is, if they ever start talking to each other."

"Maybe they're talking now."

"I doubt it. Whenever we get back, Peter's always in his room studying and Amy is upstairs baking."

"Well, all I know is, if the Lord intends for them to get married, they will—with or without your help." She grinned up at him.

"All right, all right, Mrs. Carlson. I give up. No more matchmaking."

"That's better." Martha Carlson nestled closer into the arms of her husband.

"Maybe I'll just have a talk with that boy on the art of good conversation."

"John!"

He laughed. "Just seeing if you were still listening, dear."

◆　◆　◆

A sudden loud pounding on the front door of the chapel brought Peter quickly to his feet from his curled-up perch on the little cot where he had been studying his Bible.

"Coming," he called as the pounding continued. He hoped Amy hadn't been frightened by it. Very seldom did anyone knock at the mission after dark, and if they did, it usually meant trouble. Peter knew to be cautious in opening the door and to keep himself hidden from any light.

"Yes?" he asked hesitatingly as he cracked the door open to a narrow slit. "Who is it?"

"Does a Miss Richardson live here?" The voice was that of a young boy.

"Why do you want to know?" questioned Peter skeptically.

"A boat from Africa came to port today, sir. There was a package on board for her."

"You have the package with you now?"

"Yes, sir."

"I'll take it for her, thank you." Peter reached his hand out.

"Just a minute, sir. That will be a dollar."

"A dollar! Isn't that a little high?"

"No, sir, not if you want the package."

"Just a minute. I thought the port usually sent a notice by mail to come and pick up packages."

"Well—ah—sometimes, sir." The voice outside was becoming decidedly nervous.

"You stole that package, didn't you?" Peter's voice was stern, yet kind.

"Please, sir, I don't want no trouble. You just give me a dollar and I'll be on my way."

"Just a minute." Peter lit the gas lantern that hung beside the chapel door. "I don't have a dollar, but if you'll come in for a few minutes, maybe we can make a deal," he said kindly as he pulled open the door.

"Ah, I don't know, sir."

"It's all right. I won't hurt you."

"Well—I guess so."

Trembling, the boy entered and took a seat on one of the pews that Peter motioned to him to sit down on. He was about thirteen, very thin, his clothes ragged and dirty.

"You said we can make some sort of deal?" he asked haltingly as he glanced fearfully about the room.

"That's right. But first of all, I'd like to know who I'm making deals with. My name's Peter. What's yours?" Peter extended his hand.

The boy hesitated a moment, then replied, "I'm Joe."

"Well, Joe, nice to meet you." Peter shook his hand warmly. "Now," he said, seating himself beside the boy, "I'll tell you what the deal is. I don't have a dollar—money's as scarce around here as it is anywhere else. But I can give you something else that I think you could use."

Joe said nothing, but stared straight at Peter, his eyes still wide with fear.

"How long has it been since you've eaten, Joe?"

There was a slight pause. "I guess a day or two, sir."

"That's what I thought. How would you like a nice hot meal in exchange for the package, and" Peter looked him over carefully, "maybe some new clothes to go with it?"

"You mean it, sir?"

"I sure do! Follow me."

Still leery of Peter's motives, the boy cautiously followed him up the stairs to the apartment.

Peter knocked quietly on the door. "Amy, it's me, Peter."

"Peter? What was the knocking I heard downstairs?" Her voice was a frightened whisper.

"There's a boy here who needs a good hot meal, and a package for you from Africa."

"From Africa!" At the sound of the knocking downstairs, Amy had taken every precaution and bolted the upstairs door. But now the bolt slid quickly out of its place and the door opened.

"From Africa? Oh, let me see it!"

Joe clutched the package tighter.

"I—uh, promised him a good hot meal first," Peter announced sheepishly.

"Oh, of course. How about some stew?" she asked haphazardly as she dashed frantically around the small kitchen in search of the needed plates and utensils.

"Stew would be just fine, ma'am," answered Joe as he cautiously lowered himself onto the chair that Peter had motioned to.

"How about some home-made bread to go with it?" offered Peter as Amy began heating up the leftover stew.

"Yes, sir. That'd be just fine!" Joe was beginning to see that he could trust his new-found friends, and a smile slowly spread across his face, though he still clung to his prized package.

"There!" exclaimed Amy when everything was finished, "and here's some butter."

Joe said nothing, but eyeing the food hungrily, he quickly dropped the package to the table and began shoveling in the stew.

Amy grabbed the bundle and ran over to the sofa, unwrapping as she went.

Peter watched them both amusedly.

When the parcel had at last been unraveled and its precious contents revealed, Amy let out a squeal, "David! Oh, I knew David would come through. Good, old, faithful David!" She then hugged the contents to her heart and suddenly burst into tears, then dashed into the Carlson's bedroom and shut the door behind her. Joe, who had hardly taken time to breathe, now stopped eating for a moment and looked inquisitively at Peter.

"Your guess is as good as mine, Joe," he laughed. "I guess that's a woman for you—unpredictable—something makes them happy, so they cry." Peter scratched his head and shrugged his shoulders, while Joe resumed his eating.

"Have some more, Joe?"

"Yes, sir. That sure is mighty fine stew!"

"Thank you, Joe. I'll give your compliments to the chef."

When Joe had at last finished, Peter sat down beside him and, pushing the dinner dishes away, said, "Joe, we've got a clothing barrel downstairs that just might have something your size in it."

A wide grin settled over the boy's grimy face.

"But first, I'd like to talk to you for a few minutes." The grin faded away as the old look of fear returned. "Don't worry now, Joe. I'm not going to turn you over to the authorities." The boy breathed a sigh of relief. "But I am going to talk to you about what you did, Joe."

"I know I done wrong, sir, but I couldn't help it."

"You couldn't?"

"No, sir. I had to get some money for food, sir. Ain't got a job—not many around."

"Do you have a family, Joe?"

"No, sir. I've been told my Ma died givin' birth to me, and that I have a Pa somewhere, but I ain't never even seen him."

Peter's heart reached out to the young boy. Once again he felt remorse for feeling so sorry for himself when others had much greater burdens.

"Well, Joe, I'm afraid I can't help you find your family, but I can introduce you to another family. The Father of this family is

95

so very kind that He lets anyone become a member of His family, no matter who they are or what they've done."

"He does?" Joe's eyes became wide with amazement. "He must have one awful big house!"

"Oh, He does, Joe. Bigger and more beautiful than anything you've ever seen!"

"Have you ever been there, sir?"

"No, not yet, but I'm going there someday. You see, He's my Father, too."

Joe gave Peter a doubtful look as if to say that he had gone mad. Peter walked over to the sofa and returned with Rev. Carlson's Bible.

"Do you know what this is, Joe?"

"No, sir."

"It's a Bible. Ever heard of it?"

"Yes, sir, I've heard about it."

"Can you read, Joe?"

"No, sir." Joe hung his head in shame. "I even had to get someone to tell me what the name and address was on that package."

"Well, that's all right. I'll read it to you, Joe." Peter sat down beside him again and opened the Book to Romans. "This Book, Joe, is a love letter to the world. God sent it. In it He tells us all about ourselves; how wicked and sinful we are and how we deserve to be punished by spending eternity in Hell. Did you ever hear about that, Joe?"

"Yes, sir, I've heard some about it. Least

I know there's a Hell."

"It's a terrible place, Joe, full of fire that never goes out, and darkness, and crying."

"And that's where God says we have to go?"

"That's where He says we deserve to go for our sin—like stealing and lying ... "

Joe lowered his eyes.

"You're not the only one who has ever sinned, Joe. I'm just as guilty as you are."

"Oh, no sir, you're good."

"No, Joe, I'm a sinner just like you. It says right here in Romans 3:23, 'For all have sinned and come short of the glory of God.' That means me, too. Everyone that has ever lived or ever will live is included, except for God's perfect Son. But that's not the end of it. You see, Joe, over here it says, 'For the wages of sin is death.' That's talking about our punishment in Hell. 'But the gift of God is eternal life through Jesus Christ our Lord.' You see, Joe, God is not willing that any should perish. He doesn't want people to spend forever and ever in Hell. He wants them to come to His home, Heaven, and live with Him forever."

"I'd like that, too, sir. I don't want to go to that other place."

"You don't have to, Joe. God made a way for anyone who wants to go to Heaven and spend eternity with Him. He sent His only Son, Jesus, to die on the cross for our sins.

When He died, He took our punishment, yours and mine, Joe, so that if we ask Him to save us and come into our hearts, He will. Then we don't have to pay that awful punishment."

"You sure He'll do that for me?"

"If you ask Him."

"I—I'd like to, but I don't know how."

"Just pray—talk to God. Tell Him you know you're a sinner and that you want Him to come into your heart and make you clean and save you."

"I guess I can do that."

Peter bowed his head and closed his eyes, giving the young boy an example to follow. Timidly Joe began praying. "Lord, You know I'm a sinner of the worst sort. I ain't done nothing but bad for as long as I can remember. This man here, I think he said his name was Peter, he says You love me and can save me. Please, Lord, I ask You to do that just now. Thanks."

Peter glanced up in time to see Joe wipe a tear away from his eyes. He was convinced that the decision was genuine.

"Well, Joe, how about some new clothes?"

"Yes, sir!"

Joe followed Peter down to the back "cell" which had been transformed into a pleasant bedroom with Mrs. Carlson's heirloom quilt and hand-braided rug, not to mention the other "homey" objects that had been placed decoratively around the room by a motherly hand, to the big clothing barrel in the corner. Peter opened it carefully and the two began rummaging through its contents until they found just the right thing.

"Joe," remarked Peter after Joe had donned his new outfit, "you look quite handsome."

"Thank you, sir." It was obvious from his proud stance that Joe was also rather pleased with his appearance.

"If you come back tomorrow, I'll help you find a job. And maybe we can even see about teaching you how to read. Would you like that?"

"Yes, sir! I'd really like that!"

"Fine. We'll see you then."

The two shook hands and Joe departed, leaving the chapel just as the Carlsons were entering.

"Well, what was that all about?"

"It's a long story, sir, but it's got a very happy ending."

"Well, wonderful! Come on upstairs and we'll have some tea and you can tell us all about it."

Peter and the Carlsons ventured upstairs and found Amy seated on the sofa still clutching the contents of the surprise package. The tears, however, had been replaced by a broad smile. Peter was sure that he would never understand this girl that

99

so intrigued him.

"Well," remarked Rev. Carlson jovially, "and what great story have you got to tell? The two of you didn't get engaged while we were gone, did you?"

"John!" Exasperated and embarrassed, Mrs. Carlson hurriedly retreated to the bedroom with their wraps while Peter hung his head and shifted his foot nervously back and forth across the floor, and Amy blushed a lovely pink.

"Humph! I guess not," murmured the Reverend, a little embarrassed at himself. "Well, ah, whose story should we listen to first?"

"Amy's."

"Peter's," they both said in unison.

Rev. Carlson scratched his head in perplexity.

"I think Amy ought to go first, sir, since I'm really in the dark about her story as much as you are."

"Oh? This should be interesting." Mrs. Carlson sat down beside Amy on the couch while Mr. Carlson chose his favorite chair and Peter sat down at the table.

"Begin," said Rev. Carlson.

Shyly, Amy began the story with the thumping on the outside door, Peter filling in the details that she was not aware of.

"Then I opened the package, and—"

"She started crying."

"Crying?" said Mrs. Carlson sympathetically. "Oh, my dear."

"Oh, it's all right, Mama Carlson. I was happy."

"Women," said the minister, glancing at Peter and shaking his head.

"Oh, Mama and Papa Carlson, Peter, it's a picture of Mother and Daddy!" Again the tears began streaming down her face.

"Oh, my dear." Mrs. Carlson hugged Amy tightly until she had regained her composure.

"David sent it. He said it was the only thing the attackers had left intact. He said he knew I'd want to have it. I just knew David couldn't have been one of the ones that—that—killed them. I just knew it!" Amy cried some more.

"I'm sorry, Amy," Peter began, "I should have been of more comfort. I didn't know."

"That's all right. What you did tonight was of far greater importance. Besides, I just needed to be by myself for a while anyway."

"Oh, Amy dear, may I see it?" Mrs. Carlson gently took the picture. "It's beautiful! And you're in it, too." She handed it to her husband. "Isn't it a good picture of them, John?"

"It's wonderful! Looks just like them."

"It was taken shortly before we went back to Africa a little over three years ago. I was so afraid I'd never see it again, but

101

David sent it. May the Lord bless him."

"David. He was your father's first convert in Africa, wasn't he?"

"Yes, Papa Carlson, and he proved so faithful through the years. I just couldn't believe that he had anything to do with the uprising. Of course, since I wasn't there at the time of the attack, I had no way of knowing. Things happened so fast."

"I know, honey." Mrs. Carlson gently brought Amy's head to rest on her own broad shoulders. "Bless your heart, you've been through so much, dear."

"Oh, I'll be fine, Mama Carlson. I'm just so thankful that I'll see them again one day and that—that I can have this much of them with me now." She sighed contentedly and leaned her full weight against her new mother.

"Well, Peter, how about your story?" said Rev. Carlson after clearing his throat.

"I guess you heard most of it, sir, except the best part."

"Continue."

"Well, Joe got saved!"

"You don't say! Looks to me like you are cut out to be a preacher, son. Only thing you need now is a wife."

Chapter 16

Peter hadn't dared to look at Amy much since the night of Rev. Carlson's obvious hints. He found it hard to work with the minister also. He wasn't really upset at him. In fact, he thought it had been rather funny. Still, he wasn't sure he enjoyed being the brunt of a joke that really wasn't a joke, of having something that meant so much to him treated so lightly. He wondered what Amy thought about it. He did not have to wait long to find out.

Amy and Peter had been given the job of sorting through clothing that had come in from various charitable people to be distributed among Philadelphia's poor. No doubt Rev. Carlson had purposely planned for the two to be alone so they could talk. But, as usual, they remained silent, until finally, after about an hour, Amy spoke.

"Peter?"

"Yes?"

"Are you thinking what I'm thinking?"

"Depends on what you're thinking." He tried to sound casual and self-assured, but his heart was beating so wildly that he was afraid she would hear it.

"I'm thinking that Papa Carlson is up to his old tricks." She smiled.

"You mean putting us together like this?"

"Mm-hmm."

"I think you're right." He smiled back, then grew serious. "Look, Amy, I'm really sorry about the things he's said."

"Oh?"

"I mean, I know it must be embarrassing to you—"

"He means well—"

"Oh, I know he does, and well, it is sort of funny, I guess."

Amy chuckled to herself and the two worked on in silence for about another half an hour.

"Peter, the only reason I said anything about it is . . . well . . . because I knew you felt badly, and I didn't want you to think that I felt badly. I mean, I didn't want you to feel badly on my account. What I mean is—"

"That's okay, I know what you mean." He smiled at her again. Her return smile sent his heart to dancing. Oh, how much he wanted to talk to her, to tell her how he felt, but the words stuck painfully in his throat.

Finally, he managed to blurt out her name.

"Yes, Peter?"

"Are-are you sure it doesn't make you

feel badly?"

"What?"

"The things Rev. Carlson says."

"Yes, I'm sure." There was a long pause. Amy took a deep breath. "Does it make you feel badly?"

"What?"

"You know."

"Oh, no, that is—What I mean to say is—"

"Well, hurry up and say it, son, before you forget what it is," Rev. Carlson chuckled from the stairway where he had just appeared. Peter blushed and looked away.

"Sorry. I'll let you continue. I just came down to tell you two that it is time for lunch. But don't let me rush you. Go ahead and finish what you were going to say. I'm leaving."

Peter continued to look away from Amy after the old man had disappeared.

"I'm sorry, Peter. He really does mean well."

"I know."

"Shall we go up to lunch?"

Peter nodded numbly and Amy started past him to go up the stairs. Before he realized what he was doing, he had grabbed her arm.

"No, wait. I love you, Amy."

Peter released his grip and stood silently, stunned by his own boldness. Amy smiled sweetly and gazed bashfully into his eyes.

"And I love you, too, Peter."

Chapter 17

They agreed that it should be a Christmas wedding. Christmas was Amy's favorite time of year, and Peter could hardly deny that even the slums of Philadelphia took on a festive air carpeted in its soft, silvery blanket of snow.

There was much to be done in a short amount of time. Martha and Amy spent countless hours stitching on the white muslin wedding gown, adding flourishes of ruffles and any bits of lace that they could scrounge from the mission barrel, while Peter and Rev. Carlson labored over the order and content of the service.

"I'd like it to convey a salvation message, sir. Is that possible?"

"Why, you sound more like a preacher every day," Rev. Carlson chuckled. "Of course, it's possible. Marriage is a symbol of Christ and the church. There's nothing that lends itself more readily to a salvation message than a wedding."

Of necessity, it would have to be a simple service. The guests would include those that regularly attended the chapel and anyone else who happened to come by.

They were indeed bright and sunny days full of laughter, love, and dreams. But as the day of the wedding approached, a dark cloud settled over the little mission.

Peter had become moody and irritable, retreating to the seclusion of his room at every opportunity.

Amy noticed the change in him, though she tried to push the haunting and fearful thoughts from her mind. Perhaps she had said something wrong. Perhaps he would have rather waited until later. Perhaps he had changed his mind.

The Carlsons also noticed the difference in his behavior.

"He wouldn't back out now, would he?" the Reverend asked his wife as they were out on one of their Thursday night buggy rides.

"No, I don't think he would," she replied quietly.

"It would break that poor girl's heart. Why, I've never seen a girl so in love with a fellow. Yet, if he has doubts—"

"I don't think he has any doubts, dear."

"Well, he certainly is acting awfully strange for a boy that's about to get married!"

"Not really, dear—"

"I certainly never acted like that before we got married. I may have been a little nervous about the thing. I mean, after all, it's a big step. It's a decision you have to live with the rest of your life."

"You make it sound like a jail sentence, dearest." She smiled sweetly at him.

"You know what I mean. I don't like it. If only I could figure that boy out. He's as unpredictable as the weather!"

Martha Carlson giggled. "He's not as unpredictable as you think."

"I suppose you know what's eating away at him."

"I think so," came the quiet reply.

"Well?"

"I'm surprised you hadn't thought of it, dear, although I'm sure you would have eventually."

"Now, Martha Carlson, don't go to complimenting me. Just tell me what's on your mind. I'm determined that something's got to be done about this before Amy really gets hurt."

"It has nothing to do with Amy, dear."

"Nothing to do with Amy! Well, who in the world does it have to do with?"

"His mother."

"His—now, why didn't I think of that?"

"Because you're a man, dear." She smiled.

Rev. Carlson gently squeezed his

wife's hand.

"What would I do without you?" he whispered tenderly.

"I'm not sure," she chuckled.

"Have you talked to him about it?"

"No, I can just tell."

"How?"

"The same way you could tell that Peter and Amy would be married someday. I just can. Perhaps it's a mother's heart."

"You do have a mother's heart, dear. Even though the Lord never blessed us with children of our own."

"He has blessed us, dear, more than I could ever have imagined or hoped for."

"I'm glad you feel that way, Martha."

"I've seen beyond the pained look on his face into his heart. It's torn, John—torn between returning home to beg his step-father into allowing his mother to attend his wedding, and the results of such an undertaking."

"I can't imagine how hard it must be for him. Both of my parents were dead when we got married, but his—"

"It's as if his mother were dead and alive at the same time. He hasn't mentioned her much in the last few months, but I know it's a constant grief to him. It has to be."

"I'll talk to him when we get home."

"What will you say?"

"I'm not sure, Martha. If it were me, I'd

109

risk the consequences."

"So would I."

"I need wisdom, Martha. Let's pray together about it."

◆　　◆　　◆

The knock at the door startled Peter, who had been deep in thought over a passage in Romans.

"Yes?"

"It's me, son," came Rev. Carlson's deep voice. "May I come in?"

Peter opened the door and the minister entered.

"I—ah—thought we might have a little talk."

"A talk, sir?" Peter shifted his eyes nervously to the floor.

"Yes. I thought it might lighten the load."

Peter met the minister's kind, sympathetic eyes. "Won't you sit down, sir?" He motioned to the only chair in the room. Peter seated himself on the cot.

"Peter, I don't mean to pry. You know that. I only want to be of help, if I can."

"I know that, sir, but I'm afraid the only thing that can help now is prayer. I already sent mother a letter."

"Well, then Martha was right."

"Sir?"

"Nothing, son. Continue. You sent your

mother a letter about the wedding?"

"Yes, sir."

"But what about your stepfather? Won't he—"

"Burn it? No sir. Not if he doesn't see it, which I pray that he won't. I sent it to Nanna through Joe. I told him he was to give it to no one else. He returned only an hour ago and said that the letter was safe within her hands. If anyone can get it to mother without 'him' seeing it, it will be Nanna."

"Well, then, we will hope and pray for the best."

Chapter 18

Dear Peter,

Your mother died suddenly yesterday. The funeral will be tomorrow at two.

Love,
Nanna

Peter stared blankly at the note that had just been handed to him. A lump grew in his throat. His head throbbed. "No . . . no, I won't believe it! He did this to me as a trick! It can't be! He just wants to torture me! I won't believe it! I won't!" He stared angrily at the note, then ripped it into tiny pieces and scattered them on the floor. "No!" The tears coursed down his cheeks unabated. He was thankful he was alone. Through blurred vision he gaped at the strewn paper.

"What if it's not a trick? What if she is—" The word caught in his throat. Passionately he began gathering the tattered pieces, then held them tightly in his hand and clutched them to his heart. "Mother! Oh, my dear mother!" He sank to his knees and buried his head in his arms on the bench in front of him.

"No! It's not true!" He pounded the bench with his fist. "It is a trick! It's just like him. He probably saw the letter and decided he'd get even with me for breaking his command. He thought he'd lure me to a 'funeral' and then when I set foot on his property he'll . . . "

He stared again at the torn bits of paper. The one on the top of the pile contained one word: died. "But what if it is true? My mother—my poor, dear mother . . . dead." He rose quickly. "I must see her! I'll risk it. I have to."

He went quickly before anyone had returned home. The sky was already beginning to darken when he reached Elm Street.

◆　◆　◆

Tethering the horse a block away from the parsonage, Peter quietly slipped through the street into the back alley. Once behind the parsonage, he glanced furtively about him, then scaled the stone fence into the garden. Cautiously, he made his way to the kitchen door and gently pushed it open, relieved to find that someone had oiled the once squeaky hinge. Stealthily, he sneaked inside, scarcely daring to breathe.

Kathryn was over by the fireplace stirring something in the big brass kettle.

"Nanna," he whispered hoarsely.

Aunt Kathryn turned towards the voice. She seemed to have grown ten years older overnight. Her face was haggard and taut.

"Peter? Is that really you?"

"Yes, Nanna, it's me."

"Oh, my dear, I knew you'd come."

"Then—then it is true?" He choked back a sob.

Tears fell from the large sunken eyes. "I'm afraid so."

"Oh, Nanna!" He fell into her arms, and the two hugged each other tightly, sobbing on each other's shoulder. "How did it happen, Nanna?" Peter asked when he had gained his composure.

"No one really knows for sure, Peter. Your mother had been having dizzy spells ever since you left. I found her. " Her eyes widened fearfully at the memory of the horrible scene. "She was lying at the bottom of the front stairs—dead." Kathryn drew a handkerchief from her apron pocket and wiped the fresh tears from her eyes. "The doctor says she must have been at the top and fainted. At least he thinks the fall is what killed her. Poor dear. If only I'd heard her fall —if only someone had been there to catch her, but no one was around when it happened."

Peter took a deep breath. "Please don't blame yourself, Nanna. She's better off now, anyway. I just wish I could have seen ... Where is she?"

"In the front parlor, dear. She looks so pretty and peaceful."

"She is peaceful now. She's with the Lord and Papa. You think it's safe to go in?"

"I can't say, Peter. You're taking a terrible risk just being here. I didn't know if I should send for you or not, but I thought you ought to know."

"You did the right thing, Nanna. He wasn't planning on notifying me then, was he?"

"No. That man! If he weren't my brother's son—he blamed you all along for her dizzy spells. He'd probably like to blame her death on you, too, I just don't understand him, Peter. I'm so sorry, dear, that all this has happened to you. I just wish there were something I could do. Perhaps I should go with you to the parlor and be a look-out."

"No, Nanna. I'd rather you stay here. I don't want you to get into trouble. Besides, I—I'd like to be alone with her for a while."

"I understand, dear. Most likely he's locked himself in his study tonight anyway, since it's Saturday."

Peter nodded silently and started for the hallway door. "There's just one other thing I'd like to ask you, Nanna."

"Yes?"

"Did—did mother find out about the wedding?"

"Yes, dear. I managed to sneak the note to her. She was so pleased. It was a great comfort to her heart that you'd found a nice girl. She—she was hoping to come."

"Does he know anything about it?"

"If he does, he's never mentioned it, so I guess she was able to keep it a secret from him."

"Good." He took another deep breath. "I guess I'd better hurry. The sooner I can leave, the better."

Kathryn nodded sadly.

Peter opened the door and tip-toed down the hall to the parlor, watching carefully in every direction as he went. He was almost afraid his stepfather would hear his pounding heart.

When he finally reached the parlor door,

he was forced to lean his full weight against the jamb to keep himself from falling. There she was—so beautiful, so pure, so dear—just as if she were still alive. He could hardly feel his leaden legs moving him across the room to the side of the casket. His arms and neck tingled. He fell to his knees beside the mahogany box and wept unashamedly over the lifeless form.

"Mama—oh, Mama! If only you could talk to me!" Tenderly, he stroked her golden hair. "I don't understand, Mama. I don't understand why all this had to happen." He gently picked up a limp, cold hand and pressed it between his warm ones. "But one day we'll both understand, won't we, Mother? One day we'll be together again, you and me and Papa. And no one will be able to take that from us. There will be no heartaches, no tears, no death."

He rose to his feet, and brushing the tears from his eyes, stooped over and affectionately kissed the pallid cheeks. "I love you, Mama."

"Well, now, isn't that touching!"

Peter jumped at the sound of the sarcastic voice and backed away from the casket. His heart seemed to be in his throat and his legs were like dead weights.

"I thought you'd come, boy, but I expected to see you at the funeral like a respectable person, not sneaking around a man's house at night."

"I didn't exactly want to be arrested in front of all those people, sir," Peter answered with a courage that he knew was not his own.

"So, you do remember my 'promise,' do you?"

"Yes, sir, I remember, but I didn't think you'd be so heartless as to deny me a few minutes alone with her."

"Humph! You *are* sentimental."

"She was my mother!"

"And she was my wife! And I loved her!"

"No! No, you couldn't have loved her! Not when you took the dearest thing she had in life away from her."

"I was the dearest thing she had in life, boy! Not you! You with your stupid notions and Bible quoting. I gave her everything a woman could want—clothes, servants, money. She loved me, not you!"

Rev. Mooring had moved closer to Peter with every word, yet Peter remained motionless. He should be hating this man in front of him, but instead he felt a deep pity welling up within his soul for this miserable creature.

"I feel sorry for you, sir."

Although Peter had said the words with true heart-felt compassion, he knew the insulting slap would come.

"Get out of my house!"

Peter walked obediently over to the door

that led into the hallway and back to the kitchen. He paused for a moment and looked compassionately at his stepfather. "I love you, sir, and I'll pray for you."

"Save your prayers for yourself!" Rev. Mooring roared, picking a figurine up from the round end table and hurling it across the room at Peter, who managed to evade the blow, escaping to the safety of the hallway as the figurine shattered against the parlor wall.

Peter made his way quickly to the kitchen. Kathryn was standing just inside the door.

"I heard, dear. I'm so, so sorry."

"No, Nanna, don't be sorry for my sake." He shook his head sadly. "He's the one to be pitied."

Kathryn silently agreed.

"And what about you, Nanna?"

"Me, dear?"

"What are you going to do now?"

"I don't really know. I thought I'd stay around until the funeral. After that I don't know. I can't live anymore in the same house with that man—not after all he's done, and not without your dear mother, even if he is the only blood relation I have."

"Come to the chapel, Nanna."

"Oh, no, Peter, I couldn't do that. You have a life of your own to start."

"Please, Nanna." The deep blue eyes

pleaded with her as they had when he was a child trying to get his own way. "I need you, Nanna. You're all I have of—"

"But what about your wife, dear? She won't want an old woman around. There isn't enough room in that place for everyone, Peter."

"She'll love you, Nanna, just as I do. Please say yes."

The blue eyes were pleading again. She never had been able to refuse them. "All right, dear, if that's what you want."

"It's what I want, Nanna, and I believe it's what mother would have wanted too."

Chapter 19

Christmas Day! The little chapel was alive with greenery, candles, and ribbon. A low buzzing swept through the small auditorium as Peter stepped out of the back room with Rev. Carlson and Joe, the best man.

Kathryn smiled sorrowfully at Peter from her seat of honor in the front row and hoped he hadn't noticed the tear that had escaped and even now trickled down her worn cheek.

Mrs. Carlson began the majestic wedding march as everyone rose to their feet and the beautiful bride entered the chapel and proceeded down the aisle to meet her love. The radiant smile on her face filled the vacuum in the soul of the waiting groom. God had not left him comfortless. Peter thought he had never seen a girl as lovely and sweet as his bride, his own dear Amy.

The congregation seated themselves as Peter and Amy joined hands and turned towards the minister. Mrs. Carlson quietly slipped away from the piano and took her place beside the bride, taking the part of both mother and matron of honor.

"Dear friends, we are gathered here together in the sight of God and in the presence of these witnesses to join this man and woman in the holy estate of matrimony, which is an honorable estate, instituted by God in the time of man's innocence, and signifying to us the mystical unity that exists between Christ and the Church."

Peter's hand tightened around Amy's soft one.

Rev. Carlson looked intently into the eyes of his young friend. Somehow Peter felt as though he were gaining more than a wife.

"Peter, wilt thou have this woman to be thy wedded wife; to live together after God's ordinance in the holy estate of marriage? Wilt thou love her, comfort her, honor and keep her, in sickness and in health, and forsaking all others, keep thee only unto her so long as ye both shall live?"

Peter looked down into the smiling brown eyes of his love. His voice was low and full of emotion. "Yes, sir, I will."

"Amy, wilt thou have this man to be thy wedded husband; to live together after God's ordinance in the holy estate of marriage? Wilt thou love him, honor him, keep him and obey him, in sickness and in health, and forsaking all others, keep thee only unto him as long as ye both shall live?"

Amy, still returning Peter's loving gaze, whispered ever so softly, "I will."

Turning towards each other, Peter took Amy's free hand gently in his. This had been the part of the ceremony that had most frightened him—he was sure he would forget the vows he had memorized. But now, as he stood on the threshold of matrimony, ready to become one with this girl that had captured his heart from the moment he had laid eyes on her, he forgot his nervousness, and thought only of how much he loved her, of how much she filled the emptiness in his soul, of how he would cherish her through the years, each year drawing them closer together; sharing, caring, ministering to-gether, "till death do us part."

It was Amy's turn now. As she tenderly spoke her words of promise, her mind joyfully pictured the future. Theirs would be a marriage such as her parents' had been, such as the Carlsons had; one of mutual love and understanding, of giving of oneself for the other's benefit—a life of laughter, love, and service, "till death do us part."

Rev. Carlson motioned to Joe to produce the rings. They were simple, inexpensive rings—gifts from the Carlsons, who had taken all the money they had saved up in their little nestegg for sickness or emergencies.

"We read in God's Word that when God made a covenant with Noah, that He set a rainbow in the sky as a token of that covenant. And so we may learn that it is well for us, when we enter into a solemn agreement with one another, to set aside some reminders of the things that we have promised. And what token do you present of your marriage covenant?"

"These rings, sir."

"These rings which you have selected to be a token of the covenant between you represent several things: the precious metals represent the precious ties that will unite you as husband and wife; these rings, which are endless until broken by some outside force, are to us a symbol of the union of hands and hearts, which must continue until broken only by death; and they are a reminder of the promises you have pledged one to another this day."

Peter took the ring which Joe had handed to him and placed it tenderly on Amy's finger. "With this ring, I thee wed, and with my worldly goods, I thee endow. In the name of the Father, and of the Son, and of the Holy Spirit."

Amy now placed a ring on Peter's finger and repeated the words, although it was hard for both of them not to laugh at the part about the worldly goods, since neither one had any nor expected to have much in the future.

Peter and Amy turned back towards Rev. Carlson as they had practiced, and Rev. Carlson began his "sermonette."

Finally, the moment arrived, that magical moment that every prospective bride eagerly awaits; the moment when she takes her husband's last name, when they are no longer two personages, but one in Christ.

"I now pronounce you man and wife."

Mrs. Carlson was back at the piano and the happy couple proceeded joyfully down the aisle, smiling at their friends as they went.

One by one the people greeted the new husband and wife with many congratulations and well-wishes until all had departed and the little chapel looked quite lonely.

"Well, son," remarked Rev. Carlson

teasingly, "any regrets?"

"No, sir!" Peter smiled lovingly at Amy who had not released his hand from her grip through the entire wedding and congratulations.

"May God bless you, dear!" Aunt Kathryn managed to say brokenly through her now free-flowing tears. "And you, too, honey." Kathryn put her arms around Amy and gave her a squeeze. "You'll make a fine wife for Peter. His mother would have been so proud." She then retreated hastily upstairs for a good cry.

"Poor dear," said Mrs. Carlson. "She must really have been devoted to your mother."

"Yes, she was. And mother loved her just as much. I almost think it's harder on Nanna than it is on me."

"You seem to have taken it very well, son," Rev. Carlson said proudly.

"Thank you, sir, I couldn't have done it without the Lord. Somehow I know there's a purpose in it, although I don't know what it is. But God must have had a reason for taking her now. I wish you could have seen the pained, hollow look on my stepfather's face. It's strange, but I felt sorrier for him than for me. He doesn't have the hope of seeing her again. I do."

Everyone nodded in silent agreement. The Carlsons walked hand in hand up the rickety steps to their little apartment, and Peter and Amy strolled leisurely arm in arm to the little back-room "cell," which through the efforts of Kathryn, Mrs. Carlson, and Amy had been transformed into what now seemed to Peter to be a "palace."

Chapter 20

Peter leaned back in the overstuffed chair that had been moved downstairs to his and Amy's "palace" and marveled at the changes that had taken place in his life in less than a year: his call to preach, his leaving home, his mother's death, his marriage—all passed before his mind in review.

He sighed. Those things were past. Never again could he relive any of them. This was a new year—a year of beginnings. He was on his own now, with a wife and a ministry.

Things had settled down to a comfortable routine at the mission. Kathryn had insisted on taking over all the domestic duties, leaving Mrs. Carlson and Amy free to do more extensive personal work with the women of Philadelphia's ghettos. Rev. Carlson and Peter were constantly busy during the days with preaching and teaching, aiding the sick, comforting the bereaved, and counseling the fallen.

Evenings, with the exception of Friday, Saturday, and Sunday, which were reserved for preaching services, were delightful times of quiet study around God's Word, singing of hymns and choruses, or sharing with each other the trials and blessings of the day's work. Rev. and Mrs. Carlson still had their Thursday night buggy rides, and Tuesday night had become Peter and Amy's special night out.

Although peace and happiness reigned within the walls of the little mission, conditions outside were becoming increasingly worse. Emancipated slaves continually arrived in Philadelphia by the scores even though the Emancipation Proclamation had been signed more than ten years before. Immigrants from Germany, Italy, Poland, Russia, and many other nations flooded Philadelphia's ports. Housing conditions became more and more crowded as new, poorly-constructed tenements rose overnight, wedged in between the old.

As winter turned to spring, jobs became increasingly scarce. People turned to the bottle. Children were left unattended to fend for themselves while their parents, overwhelmed by the mountainous odds against them, reveled in sinful pleasures in an effort to forget. Those fortunate enough to have jobs worked under horrible, unsanitary conditions for long hours with little pay to show for their toil.

Summer arrived, and with it, hot, sticky days that only served to increase the misery and stench of the slums. Soon, the dreaded diseases were rampant: yellow fever, small-pox, typhoid. The mission's small auditorium became an infirmary for many of Phila-delphia's poor who could not afford a doctor or had been turned away from the already overcrowded hospitals.

"Amy, would you ask Kathryn to heat some more water, please?"

"Yes, Mama Carlson. Anything else?"

"No, except we'll need clean towels and washcloths by tomorrow. Oh, and medicine. See if there's any more medicine upstairs."

Amy dashed up the rickety stairs and told Kathryn of the various needs.

"Here are some fresh cloths, honey, that I washed just today." Kathryn handed her a bundle of neatly folded towels. "I'll have some hot water ready in just a minute, but medicine? I'm afraid there just isn't any more."

"No more medicine? Mama Carlson's just about out, and you ought to see the people that are lined up outside the door wanting treatment and medicine!"

"I know, dear. I don't know what to do. Maybe we'll have to buy some more."

"But there isn't any more money, Nanna. I looked in the money crock just this morning. It's empty!"

"Now don't you worry, dear." She patted Amy gently on the arm. "Peter will know what to do when he gets home."

"But that won't be until late tonight. It's awful, Nanna! Both he and Rev. Carlson holding funeral services today, and one of them a baby!" She sat down on the couch and buried her head in her hands. "I just wish we could do more!" Tears began to course down the smooth cheeks. "It all seems so unfair!"

"Unfair?" Kathryn sat down beside her and stroked Amy's long brown hair. "What's unfair?"

"That some people have to suffer so much. Why is it, Nanna?" Amy wiped her eyes and gazed fervently at the sweet elderly lady she had come to love so much.

"I don't know, honey, but God does. And He's a whole lot smarter than we human folk are. Why do you think He allowed your mama and papa to be killed, or let Peter's dear mother die? He had a reason, I know. I've seen a big change in Peter. He's a man now. He's all grown up—overnight. Instead of worrying about himself, he's helping others who are worse off than he. Some

128

things may seem unfair to us, but then, we aren't the ones who know the end from the beginning. Someday the Lord will tell us why. Till then, we just have to trust Him."

"Oh, Nanna, I know you're right. I'm sorry. I know in my own life how the Lord used my parents' death to help strengthen me and mature me in a way that never would have been possible otherwise. The Lord does have a reason—for everything." She wiped her eyes again and smiled. "Well, I'd better hurry to Doc Marshall's before it gets dark. Maybe he's got some medicine he can loan us until we have some money."

"There now. That's more like my girl."

Kathryn watched Amy as she ran down the people-filled street, her long skirt swirling out behind her, her glossy brown hair escaping the bonnet that had fallen from her head and blowing carelessly in the breeze as she hurried to find the doctor and obtain the precious medicine.

"Nancy would have been so proud."

◆　　◆　　◆

Amy returned with bad news. The doctor was out of medicine; had been for two days. Reluctantly, Mrs. Carlson closed the mission door, turning away at least twenty untreated people.

"We'll just have to pray that the Lord sends us some more medicine." She sighed as she laid the fresh towels on the dresser in her bedroom and rejoined Kathryn and Amy in the kitchen-living room. "John and Peter should be back soon. Maybe they'll know of someplace to get some."

Amy nodded and motioned for Mrs. Carlson to come sit by her on the couch. "You look tired, Mama Carlson. Why don't you rest for a while. You've certainly earned it."

"Humph. I've done no more than anyone else in this household. The Lord sent you and Peter at the right time. John and I aren't getting any younger. I don't think we could have handled this situation alone."

Martha Carlson glanced at Kathryn who was busy setting the table for supper.

"And you, Kathryn. You're just remarkable. I don't know how you do it. You seem to work circles around the rest of us."

"Are you trying to tell me I'm getting old, Martha?" She winked at her friend. "You're no spring chicken yourself, you know."

Martha laughed. "I know, I know, Kathryn. I just wish I had half the energy that you do."

The downstairs door banged shut.

"That's John and Peter," remarked Kathryn matter-of-factly.

"How do you know, Nanna?" Amy asked wonderingly.

"Oh, I know Peter's stomach. It's just as good as one of those fancy pocket watches when it comes to supper time."

Amy and Martha laughed.

"Well, what's so funny?" asked Peter, as he and Rev. Carlson, both looking emotionally haggard, entered the room.

"We were just laughing about your stomach, dear," said Amy nonchalantly.

"My stomach! What's the matter with my stomach?" he asked, trying to sound insulted.

"Nothing, dear. It just doesn't like to miss my cooking! Never did and never will!" Kathryn smiled triumphantly as she placed the steaming bowl of stew in the center of the table. "Dinner is served."

Amy waited until after prayer to break the news about the medicine to the two men.

"I thought it would happen sooner or later," remarked the Reverend.

"Mmm. They were talking about it at the Smith's today. That's why the baby died. They couldn't get the medicine," added Peter.

Amy shook her head in sympathy. "How did they take it?"

"The Smiths? Fine. They know the baby's with the Lord."

"I'm not so sure myself that the medicine really helps anyway," continued Rev. Carlson. "I've heard of about just as many folks dying who've taken the medicine as those who haven't."

"When do you suppose it will end, Papa Carlson?"

"I'm afraid that's a question that only God can answer. At any rate, He has a purpose in it. We must do all we can and trust Him for the rest."

Chapter 21

The next morning came too early. A woman and two ragged children knocked on the door at about 6:00 a.m., only to be turned away by a regretful Peter. He and Amy decided they would go upstairs for an early breakfast and set out immediately afterwards in search of medicine.

They discovered Kathryn already aroused and diligently working at tidying up and preparing breakfast. Rather than waking the Carlsons, the three ate breakfast together, then Peter and Amy quietly hitched the horse to the buggy.

"I don't know when we'll be back, Nanna. You'll tell the Carlsons where we are?"

"Yes, dear. The Lord bless you now."

"Thank you, Nanna. Pray for us." He

squeezed her hand, then cracked the whip and they were gone.

◆   ◆   ◆

It was dark by the time they arrived home. Weary and disheartened at their futile efforts, they climbed up the stairs to break the bad news.

Upon opening the door, they sensed that something was wrong. Rev. Carlson was sitting on the couch, head in hands. Kathryn evaded their eyes and stood motionless in the corner of the kitchen. Peter glanced from one to the other. "What's wrong? Where's Mama Carlson?"

Rev. Carlson raised haggard, blood-shot eyes. Though he was looking straight at Peter, it was a glassy, vacant stare, as if he were not seeing anything at all.

"She's dead, Peter," came the hoarse whisper.

"Dead!" Amy put her hand to her mouth and bit down hard to keep from screaming. "No! No! Not Mama Carlson!" She ran to the bedroom door and flung it open. There on the bed lay a form, still and mute, covered by a white sheet.

"No! It can't be!" Peter choked back the tears. "If only we'd had some medicine!"

"No, son, it wouldn't have helped. She . . . she went too fast." Rev. Carlson buried his head in his hands and sobbed.

Peter sat down beside him, feeling absolutely helpless at lending any comfort. From the nearby bedroom he could hear his wife's weeping.

"She was around it so much—more than any of us," Rev. Carlson said to no one in particular. "I should have helped her more. I should have been able to see how tired she was. She didn't have a chance against it. It's all my fault!" He sobbed some more.

"It's not your fault, sir. When could you have helped? We were all constantly busy."

"I know, I know. If only she would have complained about it. But Martha never was one to complain. She was always so patient, so loving, so giving."

"Yes, sir, she was. I ought to know. I'm one of the ones she gave the most to." He paused thoughtfully and wiped his eyes with his shirt sleeve. "But our loss is Heaven's gain. She's probably already heard her 'well done,' sir."

Rev. Carlson nodded his gray head. "I know, and that's my one comfort. I guess I know now a little more of what you've been through in the last year, son. I hope I haven't been too hard on you."

"No, sir, you weren't too hard on me, though I must admit, at times I thought you were. But as you told me so long ago, 'All things work together for good to those that love God.' It's helped me through a lot, sir.

God's promise is still good."

◆　　◆　　◆

The next day a fresh grave was carved out of the ground in the small, nearby cemetery. A simple wooden cross stood at one end with a plaque at the bottom which read:

Martha Carlson
wife of John Carlson
"Her price was far above rubies."

Chapter 22

As summer ended, one by one the diseases abated and finally disappeared. It seemed strange that Philadelphia could still be so crowded when hundreds of its occupants had been laid to rest.

Before too long, life in the slums returned to normal. Except for the empty chairs at the dinner tables, the beds that lay vacant at night, the forsaken shoes in the corner, and the haggard, haunted looks in the eyes of people, there would have been no outward indications that the plagues had ever been there at all.

Inwardly, however, the results of the pestilence were ravaging. Almost every home in Philadelphia had been visited by the death angel. Rich and poor, young and old, all had met on common ground. Those that had died would not soon be forgotten; each had held a special place in somebody's heart.

No one could have felt the pain of the loss of a loved one more than those who dwelt within the boundaries of the little mission on Tavern Street. Kathryn missed her lovely graying friend with the soft wisps of hair always falling around her face as she scurried about on errands for her husband or comforted a crying child. Peter longed to see the sweet smile that so brightened his day. Often, his mind would flash back to the first day he had left home. There she was to greet him, attired in a long calico dress and starched white apron, looking so much like a mother. Amy remembered the strong, broad shoulder that was always ready to support her when she was so tired that she thought she would collapse, or when she simply needed to have a good cry. Somehow, Martha Carlson had always been there at the right place, at the right time.

For Rev. Carlson, the loss was so heavy that his heart ached. He and Martha had spent forty-nine long, fulfilling years together. Suddenly, he was no longer the jovial, jubilant minister who was always ready and willing to turn even the greatest of tragedies into triumph by his quick wit. He was an old man sitting in an overstuffed chair, glancing out the dingy upstairs window and sighing, longing for bygone days that could never return. He laid his head back on the chair and slept, no doubt dreaming of his youth when he had courted Miss Martha Robertson, a pretty little thing with laughing gray eyes, brownish-blond hair, and sunny smile. Before he could awaken from sleep, he was in her presence once again, and the angels sang and the Lord rejoiced that another saint had been brought safely home.

Chapter 23

Amy sighed wistfully as she walked gingerly around the upstairs apartment that had been hers and Peter's for the past three weeks. The overstuffed chair was sitting by the front window that overlooked Tavern Street. It had been moved back upstairs after Mama Carlson's death so that Rev. Carlson could enjoy his favorite seat as he read his Bible and prayed. She could almost picture him sitting there, his lips moving in silent meditation. Now and then he would part the white muslin curtains and look downward to the street below. Then he would pour out his heart before the Lord for every person he saw that needed the Savior. How she missed him. She chuckled aloud as she recalled the way he had connived to get her and Peter together. What fun-filled, exasperating days those had been!

The kitchen area with its too-small fireplace, icebox, few cupboards, and large oak table—there they had sat, first the two of them, then three, then four, and finally five. Now they were back to three. She hoped it would remain that way for many years to come. Kathryn was aging quickly, though she'd never admit her true age. Amy thought it must be close to eighty. It would be difficult without "Nanna." Her unselfish love and desire to help with the cooking and cleaning relieved Amy of those duties in order to be of more help to Peter. Besides, the thin, wiry woman who was so vivacious, yet fragile, had filled such a big vacant spot in her heart, as well as Peter's, that life just wouldn't be the same without her.

Amy ran her finger leisurely over the massive table. As she did, she could almost hear Rev. Carlson's deep, full voice as he read the Scriptures or prayed at family devotions. She could see the look of love and admiration in Mrs. Carlson's eyes as she gazed intently at her husband sitting across from her and reached for his strong hand to give it an approving squeeze.

Amy yawned and started for the bedroom. Just as she reached the door, she stopped and closed her eyes for a moment. A strange sensation overtook her. She leaned against the doorjamb and peered into the room. It too had belonged to the Carlsons. She could imagine them kneeling beside the bed praying for each member of their little congregation, sharing teasing remarks, kissing each other goodnight. Then, in her fancy, she could see a white sheet draped over a lifeless form. She closed her eyes against the scene and pressed herself harder against the doorframe. The dizziness returned. She felt tired.

She must lie down, she thought. Shaking herself out of her reverie, she lay down across the bed. She was glad that Kathryn was out shopping and Peter visiting. They would worry about her. Surely it couldn't be typhoid—that was past. She remembered Kathryn saying that the grippe was going around. Perhaps she had just been overworking herself; she had always been a frail creature. At any rate, she would not tell anyone how she felt. It would serve no purpose. She would rest. Everything would be all right; as soon as she awoke she would feel fine. She just needed rest.

But when she awoke she discovered that she was very weak. Her stomach was churning, her head spinning. By morning she was vomiting violently.

"It's the grippe, Peter. I saw Anna Forrey acting just like that the other day when I was over delivering those clothes. Why don't you let me get the doctor, dear, so you can stay right here with her?"

"All right, Nanna." Peter rubbed his hands nervously through his hair. "Tell him it's urgent!"

After Kathryn had gone, Peter returned to the bedroom. Amy was lying quietly, her face drained of all color.

"Feeling better, sweetheart?" he asked as he knelt beside her.

"Yes, Peter, thank you." The reply was weak, faint.

"Here." Peter dipped the washcloth that had been on her forehead in the dish of cool water that sat on the washstand beside the bed, rung it out, and replaced it gently on her brow. "Does that help?"

"Yes, dear." She smiled feebly.

"Do you think you can rest some, honey? It's probably the best thing for you." He hoped she didn't notice the quiver in his voice.

"Yes. I'm so tired, Peter."

He kissed her pallid cheeks and walked

quietly out, shutting the door behind him.

His Bible lay on the table where he had left it the night before. Grasping it firmly, he walked over to "Rev. Carlson's chair" and knelt in front of it. "Oh Lord," he whispered, "please, please don't—" Taking a deep breath, Peter opened the Book to Romans 8:28. "All things work together for good to them that love God, to them—" He shut it quickly and clutched the Book to his heart. "Lord, I don't understand why. I was angry with You once for taking things from me. I asked Your forgiveness, and You did forgive me. I know you did. You helped me to bear mother's death and the Carlsons' but—oh Lord, must You take her also?" A tear slipped down his cheek and onto his hand. "Lord, I love her so much, so very much, Lord. Please? Nevertheless, not my will ... but Thine." Peter brushed away the tears and rose quickly. He could hear footsteps below. It must be Kathryn returning with the doctor.

◆ ◆ ◆

Doc Marshall asked Peter a few questions, then entered the bedroom and shut the door.

Peter began pacing nervously back and forth. Kathryn tried to busy herself with things in the kitchen, absentmindedly arranging and rearranging everything she could find. Peter glanced at his watch. Doc

141

had been in there for at least half an hour. They had heard no sounds at all, not even a clue as to what he had discovered.

Unexpectedly, the door creaked open and the doctor emerged.

"How is she?" Peter asked apprehensively.

"Relax, son," the doctor replied, patting him good-naturedly on the shoulder. "She's going to be fine. You can go in and talk with her if you'd like."

Peter did not wait to hear any more. He was already beside her. Kathryn tried to follow, but the doctor motioned for her to stay out.

"Amy, Doc says you're going to be all right."

She was smiling up at him, very weakly, but it was the most beautiful smile he had ever seen. She nodded her head in assent.

"Did he say what it was or how long it will last?"

"Mmm—about seven months."

"Seven months! What in the world do you have?"

"A baby."

"A—a baby?" Peter stared at her in disbelief. "You have a baby?"

"*We* have a baby, dear!"

"We have a baby! We have a baby! Nanna, did you hear that? We have a baby!"

"You don't have one yet, son." Doctor Marshall was serious now. "That girl's going

142

to need rest, and plenty of it. No housework, no mission work, just rest."

"Yes, sir!"

"She must take care of herself if she's going to have a healthy baby. Kathryn, you'll see to it that she eats properly?"

"Oh, yes, yes!" replied Kathryn ecstatically, as she ushered the doctor to the door. "Don't you worry about a thing, doctor. She'll have the best care any mama ever had. And Peter and Amy will have the most beautiful baby there ever was!"

Chapter 24

"Didn't I tell you he would be the most beautiful baby in the world?" said Kathryn as she gently laid the infant in his cradle.

"Yes, you did, Nanna," returned the proud father. "But you failed to mention that he also has the most beautiful mother in the world." Peter bent over and kissed his wife.

"Oh, Peter," Amy sighed contentedly.

"Have you decided yet what name you like best? He's almost two days old, you know. Poor little tyke. He really ought to have some sort of name." He smiled teasingly.

"Yes, Peter. I've finally made up my mind. We'll take your favorite name and my favorite name and put them together— Jonathan David."

"Beloved gift of God," he mused. "It's perfect. Jonathan David it is."

◆   ◆   ◆

Jonathan David was a delightful addition to the little household. He was a chubby little thing, with fat, pink cheeks and a smile that spread from ear to ear; a very good-natured baby who managed to capture the heart of everyone who met him.

◆   ◆   ◆

Time passed all too quickly. Soon, baby Jonathan was a toddler, teetering around on the two feet he had suddenly discovered, exploring his little domain, while baby Heather nestled snugly in the cradle which used to be his.

Peter was always busy, yet somehow he managed to find time for his little family. The evenings when Papa was home were very special.

"Papa, wead," demanded Jonathan on one such special evening as he thrust his tiny Gospel of John, which was the only book he owned, onto his father's lap.

"All right, son. Hop up." Jonathan

clambered onto Peter's lap and buried his head in the crook of his father's strong arm.

Amy smiled thoughtfully at the lovely picture they made, father and son together, reading God's Word. Of course, Jonathan didn't actually read, but Papa made him feel as if he did. He was daddy's "little preacher." Many times after a service in the mission auditorium, he would pull a chair over, climb up on it, and start pounding on the pulpit in front of him. "Wepent!" he would cry emphatically. The adults would chuckle at his cuteness, but Amy and Peter treasured those moments and never missed a day praying that God would really use their son one day for His honor and glory.

◆   ◆   ◆

It was Jonathan's fourth birthday. Kathryn had baked a yellow cake. Heather was sitting by the table in her highchair, pounding her tray with one fist, and with the other grasping at the cake that Kathryn had placed "just out of reach." Peter and Amy were busy in the back room wrapping up Jonathan's birthday present, while Jonathan tried to peek under the door to see what it was.

"Get away from that door, young man."

"Aw, Nanna, can't I have just a little peek?"

"Now why in the world would you want a

145

little peek? You'll spoil all your fun doing that."

"No I won't, Nanna. Honest."

"You come right over here and sit yourself down, honey. It's almost time to eat your birthday cake."

"It is? Oh, boy!" Forgetting all about the present, Jonathan quickly sat down in the chair that Kathryn had pulled out for him.

He sat there impatiently humming "Amazing Grace" to himself, until his parents emerged from their bedroom with the mysterious package. It wasn't big as he had hoped, but at least it was a present. He was eager to unwrap it, but Papa said that would have to wait until after the birthday dinner.

Jonathan hardly touched a morsel of food. He didn't feel like eating anything, except cake. And that package—there it sat directly in front of him, just begging to be opened.

Finally, the time arrived. Baby Heather must have sensed that this was no ordinary night, for she was now pounding both fists on her tray and laughing excitedly.

"Sissy wants me to open my package, Papa!"

Peter grinned at him. "All right, son. I guess you've waited long enough."

Jonathan tore the wrapping paper off in a frenzy, sending bits and pieces flying

146

everywhere. Inside was a box, and inside the box was—

"A Bible! Papa, a real Bible for me?"

"Well, it's not my birthday. Is it yours, honey?"

"No, it's not my birthday," answered Amy. "Nanna?"

"I haven't had a birthday in years, and I certainly don't intend to start now."

Jonathan laughed at their teasing. "A whole Bible all my own. Just like Papa's." He sighed wistfully and clutched the Book to his heart. "Look, Mama, it's just like Papa's!"

"Yes, dear, I know. Did you see what was inside the front cover?"

Jonathan shook his curly brown head.

"It says, 'A gift from God for our gift from God.'"

"Did God give me this? I thought it was from you and Papa."

"Well, son," Peter said, "Even though your mother and I bought it for you, it really is a gift from God. It's a gift He sent to the whole world—because He loved them. Soon you'll learn to read. When you do, you must spend some time every day reading from God's Book."

"Oh, I will, Papa. I'll start tonight!"

Peter and Amy exchanged smiles as Jonathan took his new treasure to his little rocking chair which sat in the corner by "Papa's chair," sat down, and began to carefully peruse each page.

Kathryn began clearing off the dinner dishes. Amy took Heather into the bedroom for a change, and Peter took his place beside his son and read to himself from his own Bible.

"Papa," Jonathan piped after a few minutes had passed.

"Yes, Jonathan."

"I have my own Bible now, right?"

"That's right, son."

"That means I'm a big boy now, doesn't it, Papa?"

"Yes, son. It surely does."

"Well, if I'm big enough to have a Bible, don't you think I'm big enough to be saved?"

Peter laid his own Bible quietly in his lap and looked intently at the little four-year-old. "You are if you understand what it means to be saved."

"Oh, yes, Papa. You say it every Sunday. I do bad things. Jesus died for me. He wants me to ask Him into my heart and wash away my sin."

Peter was amazed that such knowledge could come from one so young. "That's exactly right, son. Would you like to do that now?"

"Oh, yes, Papa. Will you pray with me?"

Peter nodded silently as Jonathan got down from his seat and onto his knees. No sooner had Peter joined him when he felt a

148

tiny hand slip into his. Peter grasped the hand firmly. What a joy, he thought, to share in the salvation of your own child. He had led many souls to the Savior, but none could compare with this.

"Dear Jesus, I'm a bad boy, but I don't want to be. Please come into my heart and clean it out and make me good. Amen. Oh, and thank You for my Bible. Papa says You gave it to me, even though he and Mama did. And thank You for Papa and Mama and baby Heather and Nanna. And thank You that this is my birthday. Amen."

Peter's eyes were moist. "You know, son, today you can celebrate two birthdays."

"I can?" Jonathan's eyes were wide.

"Yes—your birthday into our family, and your birthday into God's family."

"Do I get another present, Papa?" Jonathan grinned at his father.

"You've already gotten your present, son. He's in your heart, and He'll never leave you."

As Peter rose from his knees, he saw Amy smiling at him from the bedroom. She, too, had been able to share in his joy.

Chapter 25

Though the mountaintop experience lingered in his heart for many days, Peter could see a valley approaching, a valley he knew he would have to pass through.

"It's Joe, isn't it, Peter?" Amy had been brushing her long brunette hair when she had noticed her husband's troubled look reflected in the mirror before her.

"Yes, Amy, it's Joe. He hasn't been in the services for a couple of weeks, now."

"Have you been by to see him?"

"No. You know how busy I've been."

"I know, dear."

"I know he's not sick because Frederick said he's been at work every day."

"When did you talk with Frederick?"

"Last Sunday."

"Was he able to tell you anything else that would give you a clue as to why Joe hasn't been there?"

"I'm afraid so. It seems when Joe first started to work at the factory a few months ago, he was really a witness for the Lord. Some of the men started to give him a hard time about it. Those very men are now Joe's friends. Frederick says Joe hardly speaks to him anymore."

"Sounds bad." Amy laid the brush down on the dresser.

"Mmmm. The pressure must have been too great for him so he gave in to them. Anyway, I'll go by and see him tomorrow."

"You're afraid to go, aren't you dear?" Amy said sympathetically as she took his two hands in hers.

"He's just like a brother to me, Amy. If he's turned his back on the Lord, I just—"

"I know, dear. That's how I felt when I thought my father's friend, David, had been one of the ones who killed him. But it wasn't true after all, and I did all that worrying in vain."

"I know it's senseless to worry, but—"

Amy put her hand gently to her husband's lips. "I'll pray for you, Peter. God will give you grace."

Peter kissed his wife's soft hand, cradling it in his own. "God certainly knew what He was saying when He said man wasn't complete without a woman. I love you, darling."

"And I love you, Peter."

◆ ◆ ◆

"Hello?" The dingy door of the tenement apartment creaked open. "Who is it?"

"It's me, Joe. Peter."

There was no answer, but the door continued to open slowly, almost reluctantly. Peter entered cautiously, his eyes straining to get accustomed to the darkness inside. It had been Joe's voice, but it had been strange and cold, not like the Joe he knew.

"What do you want?"

Peter glanced uneasily about the room and noticed that Joe was not alone. On the floor, on either side of the door, sat two other men—no doubt two of Joe's "new friends." Peter took a deep breath and tried to sound casual. "I thought I'd come by and chat with an old friend. Do you mind?"

Joe said nothing, but shifted his eyes to the floor. One of the men rose from his position.

"You a friend of Joe's here, are you?" he asked, looking Peter over from head to foot.

"Yes, I am," Peter answered. His heart was thumping wildly. Silently, he prayed for courage. The man was tall, about six-feet-four, and very brawny. "The name's Peter— Peter Andrews."

"So, you're the good 'Reverend' we've heard so much about," the man returned sarcastically, emphasizing the word Reverend.

"That's right." Peter eyed Joe again. It was obvious that he was embarrassed at his presence.

"Well, preacher," the big man continued,

152

"anything you got to say to Joe here, you can say to us. Ain't that right, George?"

"That's right," came a voice from the corner.

A long pause followed, during which Peter did some serious thinking. How could he talk to Joe with these two present? But, he had to talk to him sometime. Perhaps these men weren't as tough as they let on. But, if they were, there was no way he would have a chance against them. Surely, Joe would not let any harm come to him.

"You'd better go," Joe said suddenly. "I ain't got no use to talk to you today."

Peter could hardly believe what he was hearing. This couldn't be the same Joe that had come to the mission as a skinny, neglected boy and had so willingly received the Savior that very night, the Joe who had been the best man at his wedding, the Joe who had worked side by side with him at the mission, counseling with a countless number of people, the Joe who had been almost like a brother—

"You heard what he said, Mister. You better git."

"Joe, I just can't believe it. What's happened to you?" Not even realizing what he was doing, Peter began walking over to his friend. Suddenly, strong hands grasped his right arm and twisted it sharply behind him, holding him fast.

"He said he didn't want to talk to you, Mister." The big man tightened his grip on Peter's arm, causing Peter to wince.

"Let him be. He don't mean nothing by it." Joe's voice was tense, strained.

"Sure, Joe. If that's how you want it."

The man slowly released his grip and shoved Peter towards the door.

"Next time, preacher, you won't get off so easy."

◆　◆　◆

Peter walked grimly home. He had been hurt, deeply hurt.

His right arm and shoulder ached naggingly, but even more pained was his pride. "How could Joe turn his back on me like that—how could he allow those bums to make a fool out of me?" he thought miserably as he shuffled down the street, oblivious to everything around him. "I gave him food, shelter, helped him find jobs, led him to the Lord. He was like a brother—we were so close. Why, Lord?" Peter lifted his face towards the sky, allowing himself to drink in the balmy breeze and warm sunlight, somehow hoping they would soothe his soul. "Where have I failed, Lord? He was so faithful—so faithful. How could he do this to me? Doesn't he know how he's hurting me?"

Peter was unusually quiet that evening. He spoke nothing of his afternoon encounter until he and Amy were alone that night in the privacy of their bedroom.

"Oh, Peter, I'm so sorry. I wish I could have been there with you."

"I'm glad you weren't. You just wouldn't believe the difference in him, Amy. How can a person change like that? How could he turn his back on his best friend?"

"Are you referring to yourself, dear, or the Lord?"

"Both, I guess."

"I know it's quite a blow to you, Peter. You've helped Joe in so many ways."

Amy lowered her gaze away from her husband's and spoke in soft, gentle tones. "Just think, if a backslidden Christian brother makes us hurt so terribly, Peter, how much more must the Lord be hurting. He died for Joe."

Chapter 26

Between all the work at the mission and the turmoil over Joe, neither Peter nor Amy had noticed how much Kathryn's health was failing. Almost daily, the pains, which had once been only spasmodic, were piercing her heart. She had been successful in hiding it to this point, turning her back to others when an attack came on, as she grasped her chest in momentary anguish, but now—

"Peter! Peter! Come quickly!" Amy's shrill cry reverberated down the stairs to the auditorium where Peter was counseling with a drunk. Knowing that Amy never raised her voice unless there was a real emergency, Peter dashed up the flight of steps without so much as saying "goodbye" to the man. The drunk rose to his feet, scratched his head, shrugged his shoulders, and staggered out the door.

"Peter, I think Nanna has fainted!"

Peter gently lifted the tiny woman and carried her to the bedroom where he laid her tenderly down on the bed, then felt for her pulse.

"It's weak, Amy. Awfully weak." Peter's face was ashen. He was panting yet from his quick trip up the stairs. "You stay here with her. Try to make her as comfortable as possible. If she wakens, don't dare let her try to get up. I'll go get the doctor."

Amy nodded her assent and quickly set about to perform her various tasks. Peter began hitching the horse to the wagon. He would have to travel to the other end of town. Doc Marshall had passed away only last year and the nearest doctor was several blocks away. The buggy would be quicker than running.

The doctor's shingle was directly ahead of him now. He quickened the horse's gait. Once there, he jumped off the buggy and hurried to the door, knocking frantically. After what seemed like hours, the door opened.

"Please, sir, are you the doctor?"

"Slow down, I can't understand what you're saying!" The man bellowed, puffing away on an elaborate pipe.

"Are you the new doctor?"

"Yes, I am, but my office hours are over for the day. You'll have to come back tomorrow." The doctor started to shut the door, but Peter pushed against it, holding it open.

"This can't wait until tomorrow! My friend needs a doctor now!"

"And just what is the matter with your friend?" the man grumbled.

"I don't know. I think she may have had a heart attack. Her heartbeat is extremely weak." Peter wished the man would quit asking questions and get into the buggy. There wasn't any time to lose.

"Well, why didn't you say so? Just a minute and I'll get my bag." He started to retreat into another room, then paused. "It will cost you extra, you know, disturbing me after office hours."

Peter had not even thought of money. How different this doctor was from Doc Marshall, who would come at a moment's call, day or night, and often leave without charging a penny.

"I can't pay you now, sir. But I will as soon as I get the money."

"Humph! I didn't think you looked like you could pay anybody anything!" he snorted, examining Peter's shabby workclothes he had worn that morning in order to do some much-needed repair work around the mission, as if he were examining one of his patients and half afraid to give his diagnosis.

"Please, sir. I'm a preacher at the mission on Tavern Street. Money is scarce now, but I promise you—"

"I'm sorry, but I have to make a living too, you know. Suppose I gave everyone special favors. I'd be in the poorhouse."

"But you'll get your money."

The door slammed shut. Peter could not believe the callousness of this man. He pounded with all his might against the door. "She may die without your help! Please! Please come! I promise you that you'll get your money!"

But all his pleading was to no avail. The door remained shut with no response from within.

Reluctantly, Peter boarded the wagon and headed for home. Wearily, he trudged up the stairs to the apartment.

"Peter?" Amy met him at the door. "Where's the doctor?"

"He wouldn't come," Peter whispered, hanging his head sadly.

"Wouldn't come? Did you tell him it was urgent?"

"Yes, I told him. He essentially said, 'No money, no service.' "

"Oh Peter! What are we going to tell Kathryn?"

"Nothing, dear," came a feeble voice from the bedroom. "I heard."

Amy glanced fearfully at Peter and followed him into the room.

"Nanna," Peter said softly, "I don't know what to say. I can go and see if I can find another doctor."

"No, Peter. It's all right. I—I don't know that they could help now, anyway. Besides, I want you here when I die."

"Die! Don't say that, Nanna! You're not going to die—not if I can help it!"

"Peter, dear, there comes a time when all must die. You preach it yourself. I'm not afraid. I ... know where I'm going." Her breathing was becoming increasingly labored. Every word she spoke was now an effort. "Just think ... I may see ... your sweet Mama ... tonight."

"Oh, Nanna." Peter sank to his knees by her bedside and sobbed. Little Jonathan, bewildered and perplexed, came and stood by his father's side and, placing his small little arms around Peter's neck, hugged for all he was worth.

Heather, imitating her brother's actions, went over to her mother who was now weeping quietly and climbed up on her lap. Amy held the little girl tightly, rocking her gently back and forth.

"Amy ... dear," Kathryn's feeble voice broke through the sound of crying. "Will you ... sing ... my favorite hymn ... for me? I ... so love to ... hear ... you ... sing, dear."

Amy lifted her tear-streaked face and met Peter's gaze, then began. "He the pearly gates will open so that I may enter in. For He purchased my redemption, and forgave me all my sin. "

"I'm ... going ... home, children!" Kathryn's face was a study: radiant, peaceful, content.

"Please ... don't cry ... for me ... any ... more. I'll ... see ... you ... again."

Kathryn's eyes closed. Her body went limp. She was home.

Chapter 27

Kathryn's parting words carried Peter and Amy through the next few trying months. "Don't cry for me any more. I'll see you again." The reassuring words echoed in their ears as often as they thought of their beloved friend.

Peter was busier than ever now that Amy had to resume household duties and could no longer do as much of the mission work as she had been accustomed to doing.

These were hard times. Money was scarce. Often they would come to the last crumb of bread in the house with no idea as to how the next meal would be provided. Always, miraculously, the Lord would somehow supply the need.

"I wish I could give you more, Amy," Peter remarked wistfully one evening after Jonathan and Heather had gone to bed. "I know you have to scrape and pinch to make ends meet. You do well, dear, with the little you have."

"What do you mean, the little I have?" Amy reproved him gently. "I have the Lord and you and Jonathan and Heather, and soon I'll have another to add to the list," she said, patting her stomach. "What more could a woman ask for?"

"I know, Amy. But ... well, I don't see how we're going to do it—not with the baby coming. I don't mean just the money, but who's going to take care of the house, make the meals—I'm so busy now as it is, I can hardly find time to take a night off."

"Jonathan's getting to be quite a little helper, dear. Why just yesterday he set the table all by himself and even made some biscuits."

"Oh, I know something will work out somehow. The Lord always supplies our needs just at the right moment. Sometimes I get to worrying and just have to talk things out."

"I know, dear." Amy looked thoughtfully at her husband. "You're still disappointed over Joe, aren't you, dear?"

"How did you know?"

"Sweetheart, a wife can read her husband like a book. We're one, remember? When you hurt, I hurt. It's as simple as that."

"I know I shouldn't let it discourage me." Peter rose from his chair and walked to the window, his back to Amy. He parted the curtains and looked out. "I thought I had turned it over to the Lord, but I guess I really haven't. I trusted Joe, Amy. I trusted him too

162

much, and when he let me down ... " He sighed. "It's affecting my whole ministry. I find it hard to work with people now. I somehow expect everyone who makes a decision for Christ to eventually turn their backs on Him and me. I guess I feel like a failure; like all my efforts are futile. I'm afraid to be hurt again."

"I know it's hard, dear. I've often wondered how the Lord must have felt the night of His trial when all of His disciples forsook Him and fled."

"Mmm. The Lord keeps reminding me of that—reminding me that my success isn't based on the results, but on my faithfulness. The results are the Lord's business." He paused, then suddenly wheeled around and shouted, "That's it! That's my problem!"

"What is?" asked Amy, startled by her husband's sudden change in mood.

"I've been thinking and acting as if all the results were dependent upon me—as if I were responsible for Joe's salvation and backsliding, and as if it's up to me to bring him back to the Lord. It's not up to me! It's up to the Lord—completely. I am only called upon to be faithful—to give out the Word. Whether it falls on stony ground, or hard ground, or thorny ground; or whether it falls on good ground and brings forth fruit—that's the Lord's business. I've been trying to do His job, and it's impossible for any human being to achieve. There was a thrill and zeal to his voice that had been missing for months. "Amy, will you pray with me right now? I'm going to give this thing over to the Lord completely."

"I'd love to, dear."

◆　◆　◆

Determined to leave the results of his ministry in the Lord's hands, Peter began to spend more time each day in prayer and less time in activity. Somehow, he seemed to accomplish just as much with less anxiety and more fruit. There were still disappointing moments—the unsaved and Christians alike still brought him many heartaches, but they were easier to bear now. He would be faithful in his task—giving out the Word— and he would allow the Lord to be faithful in His responsibility of giving the increase. The mission's little congregation noticed the difference in their preacher. His messages had more fire, more urgency. God's Spirit began to move mightily. Almost every week someone came forward for salvation or rededication. A revival had come at last.

"The devil would like nothing better than to create havoc in the church right now, Amy. We must pray for the Lord's strength to meet the test when it comes."

But the test came in a totally different area than he had expected. On February 26,

1884, Jeremy Lee Andrews was born—dead. Peter stood by his two-day-old grave, now carpeted with a soft covering of snow, and wept. "Oh, Lord," he cried, "You have required many hard things of Thy servant, but this—this is the hardest." He sank to his knees and brushed the snow off the little burial marker. "Lord, I knew a test would come. I expected it. I knew the devil would seek to defeat me. I was ready for anything, Lord ... anything ... but this!" He wiped at a fallen tear. "I must be strong, Lord. I must stand the test for the sake of my dear wife and my people that are watching me so closely. Lord, give Amy back her strength, please, and somehow ... oh, somehow, dear Jesus, work this out for Your honor and glory."

Peter returned to the mission with a heavy heart. Tomorrow was Sunday. It would have been a day of rejoicing over the birth of the pastor's new baby son. Instead, it would be a time of mourning. Many had come to the little funeral they had held in his memory. Many had offered their sympathies. News had no doubt traveled around the slum district. No doubt there would be many strange faces in the congregation; people who hadn't been there for a while, a few loving friends, and many more who would simply come to see how the preacher was "taking it." Amy was still quite ill. He would have to face them alone—and he had no desire at all to even preach.

Deciding to spend the night in prayer, Peter knelt by the old, worn-out, overstuffed "preacher's chair" which Rev. Carlson's chair had lately been dubbed. Gradually, a deep peace settled over him, and he fell asleep.

◆　◆　◆

Peter faced the next morning with renewed strength and fervor. The Lord had impressed a comforting verse upon his heart. He would preach on it that morning.

" 'I shall go to him.' These were the words of David upon the death of his son by Bathsheba. They have been comforting words to me in these last few days. 'I shall go to him.' Not only do those words remind Christians of the hope of once again seeing their beloved ones who have gone on to glory before them, but they can speak to our hearts of the hope and assurance we have of one day seeing Him, the Hope of Glory, Jesus Christ, the Son of God, Who loved us and gave Himself for us."

Peter studied each face in the audience. He could not distinguish if the concerned and intense response he was getting was conviction or mere sympathy. He had hoped that Joe would be there, stirred by the news of Jeremy's death, but he had again been disappointed.

"Perhaps there are some here today who do not have the hope of going to Him. You will never see Heaven's golden streets, never dwell in a mansion in Beulah Land, never receive freedom from death, crying, sickness, pain. Why? Because you have never received pardon from your sin through the shed blood of Jesus Christ on Calvary. My friends, the Bible says, 'Today is the day of salvation.' Tomorrow may be too late. Tomorrow we may dig your grave.

"Or perhaps you have the hope of going to Him one day, but you are afraid of that day because your garments have become soiled with the sin of the world. You are ashamed for Him to see you. You will enter Heaven's gates because you have received the Savior, but you will not hear His 'Well done.' Rather, your works will be burned up and you will be saved 'so as by fire.' What a waste, my friends."

Peter felt tears stinging his eyes. If only Joe could have heard the sermon. Peter knew the Holy Spirit was moving in hearts. He had sensed the convicting Spirit. The message had not been his own. It was the Lord's. It was bound to bring results.

"I shall go to Him. Can you say the same thing, my friend? I would like everyone to bow his head and close his eyes. We have no pianist this morning, but I am sure most of you know 'Just As I Am.' As we begin singing it, if you have a need, please . . . please come. Don't put it off."

Peter kept his head bowed during the first verse and prayed. He was almost shocked when no one came forward. He knew God's Spirit was moving. Why wasn't anyone coming forward? "Please, Lord, please work in hearts. Soften them, bend them, break them to Your will," he whispered.

They were on the last verse and still no one had come forward. Peter was about to close the service when he heard the door of the mission creak open and a shuffling of feet on the bare wooden floor. He looked up to greet the penitent.

"Joe!"

Chapter 28

Knock, knock, knock! Peter was aroused by a loud pounding on the door. Sleepily, he stumbled about the bedroom until he found his robe, then felt his way down the stairs to the door.

"Who is it?" he asked cautiously. It

reminded Peter of the first night Joe had come to the mission. His heart rejoiced as he rehearsed again in his mind the past Sunday when Joe, who had been too ashamed to come into the church, had stood outside in the cold, listening by the window until he had been compelled by God's Holy Spirit to come forward and repent of his wrong-doings, restoring his fellowship with God and man.

"Lemme in."

The slurred speech told Peter that the man was drunk. "What do you want?"

"I need a place to stay for the night."

"You realize if I let you stay here you will have to allow me to counsel with you in the morning."

"Yeh."

"And you won't be able to touch a drop of liquor the whole time you're here."

"Wha do ya think I come for? Ta dry out, thas why!"

Peter doubted the man's word, but he felt compelled to let him inside. Slowly, he opened the door. Before him stood a withered, bent-over old man, his face haggard and taut, reflecting his life of sin. The man stood squinting at Peter for a few seconds through blurred vision, then fell over in a heap in Peter's arms.

Peter shut the door and half carried, half dragged the stranger to the little back room. After laying him down on the cot, Peter felt for the man's heartbeat. It was steady. No use for a doctor—he had just drunk himself into a stupor. Peter quietly slipped upstairs again and bolted the door. He never took chances with his family whenever the downstairs room was "occupied."

The next morning Peter went down to check on his lodger, totally expecting him to be gone. There he lay, still fast asleep, his straggling gray hair falling about his face, his mouth wide open, snoring peacefully away.

At lunchtime, Peter returned with some coffee. This time his guest was sitting on the side of the cot rubbing his face with his hands and moaning.

"Here, sir, drink this." The man tried to push the cup from his lips, but Peter managed to force the hot liquid down his throat. "It will be good for you to sober up a bit."

"I don' wanna be sobered up!" the man snapped.

"That's not what you said last night."

"Humph! Who knows what I said last night. I didn't come here ta get sober."

"Then why did you come?" Something about the stranger made Peter feel ill at ease.

"I came here ta die, that's what!"

"To die?"

"You heard me! Figured I ought ta have a nice bed to lie on when I die."

170

"And who says you're going to die?" Peter was truly concerned for the man now. He took a seat by the cot.

"I know it's comin'. It's the liquor and . . ."

"And what, sir?"

"Get out!"

Peter was now completely bewildered. "What?"

"You heard me! Get out! I don' wanna see you!"

"All right," Peter answered quietly, "I'll leave, but I'll be back later. I'm here to help you, sir. I can only do that if you tell me what your trouble is."

"You'll find out soon enough," came the gruff reply.

◆　　◆　　◆

Peter tried to find some time to talk with the man every day, but still he would not open up. As the days progressed, the man's physical condition worsened, yet he would not allow Peter to send for a doctor.

"He's a strange one, all right," Peter told Amy. "I don't trust him. Be sure you and the children stay away from him."

"We will, dear. It gives me a creepy feeling just knowing he's down there."

"I know. At least he's getting the gospel every service, but if he doesn't soon open up to me and allow me to counsel with him, I'll have no choice but to turn him over to the

171

authorities. We can't keep him down there forever."

◆　◆　◆

Peter started pacing back and forth across the little "cell." The stranger who had now been with them for an entire month had taken a turn for the worse. Peter was sincerely afraid it would be the man's last day on earth.

"Look, you've got to let me send for a doctor."

"No!" The old man started to cough and sputter. Peter gave him a cool drink of water. "There's nothing a doctor could do for me now, anyway."

"Then what about the Lord. Won't you give Him a chance? You've heard me preach. You know you're on your way to Hell. Why don't you repent before it's too late?"

"I can't."

"But why? What could be holding you back from accepting Him? You're about to die! You may not have another day!"

"Doesn't matter. No one cares what happens to me now—not even me."

"I care." Peter looked earnestly and compassionately at the waste of human potential lying before him. Though the man made him feel frustrated and angry at times, he had somehow grown to love this pitiful creature.

172

"Would you care if you knew I'd killed somebody?" A hollow, haunted look filled the man's eyes.

"Yes."

"Can God forgive a murderer?"

"Of course, He can, if the murderer is truly repentant."

"Could you forgive a murderer?"

Peter paused for a moment, then nodded, "Yes."

The man caught Peter's full gaze. "Even —even if he killed your mother?"

Peter reached for the chair in front of him. His head felt light. His knees buckled.

"What did you say?" he whispered.

"You didn't recognize me, did you, boy?"

"I—I—no sir, I didn't." Peter turned his back toward his stepfather.

"Sin's taken its toll on me, boy. I'd like to ask God's forgiveness, but I can't . . . not until I have yours."

Peter stared at the wall in front of him. "I don't understand, sir. I thought mother's . . . "

" . . . death was an accident?"

"Yes, sir."

"That's what I wanted everyone to think. That's what I wanted to think." Rev. Mooring started coughing again. Peter went to his side, lifted his head, and gave him some more of the water. Their eyes met. Peter let his stepfather's head drop gently back on the pillow and turned away.

"Go on, sir."

"It was my temper, boy. I hated you; hated you because you were everything I wasn't; hated you because you reminded your mother of your father. He was a good man, and I was exactly what you said I was, boy—a hypocrite!"

Peter swallowed hard and said nothing.

"Your mother was a good woman, boy—the best there ever was. She didn't hide your wedding from me. She showed me the letter and meekly asked my permission to go." Mr. Mooring shifted his position and grunted. Peter knew he must be in a great deal of pain.

"I was angry—angry that you would have the audacity to go against my authority—angry because no matter how much I tried to push you out of my life, you kept returning, reminding me of the shell of a man I was."

"I—"

"No, boy, let me finish. I—I struck her. It was the first time I had ever hit her. I didn't realize she was so close to the staircase. She—she fell."

Peter choked back the tears that were stinging his eyes.

"I guess you had heard that I resigned the church not long afterward."

"Y-yes, sir."

"It was because of guilt. I'd started drinking ... I couldn't bear myself. I knew that soon I would be discovered unless I left then. I had to be able to leave with my dignity. You can understand that, can't you, boy?"

"Yes, sir."

"Since then I've lived in the gutter. I've tried to drown my sin, but it continues to haunt me. I can't expect your forgiveness, but I can at least ask for it."

Peter turned and faced his stepfather. The tears had now overridden their boundaries and were coursing down his face. "There was a time, sir, when I could not have forgiven you. I guess my pride was crushed. It wasn't until I saw you that last time in the parlor that I realized I needed to forgive you, to love you, to pray for your salvation. There's not a day that's gone by since that time that I haven't prayed for you, sir. Will you accept that for forgiveness?"

Peter knelt beside the bed of the dying man. "You see, sir, I really forgave you back then, though I never realized—"

Mr. Mooring grasped Peter's hand in his own trembling one. "And now I can have that peace, too. You have forgiven me. God will also forgive me. I am ready to accept that forgiveness. Will you pray with me ... " he tightened his grip on Peter's hand and smiled, "son?"